STAR DEMON!

"I am not finished with you mortals," Iblis said. "There will be another time, another place. We will meet again."

He threw out his arms and the air around him crackled with energy, then the sky over the ridge became filled with light, a bright glowing light like that of a sun going nova. Starbuck and Sheba turned away, shielding their eyes. An explosion shook the air and ground, tumbling them to the earth.

When they looked up, Iblis was gone....

BattlestaR
GALACTICA 7
WAR OF THE GODS

BY GLEN A. LARSON AND NICHOLAS YERMAKOV

Based on the Universal Television Series
"Battlestar Galactica"
Created by Glen A. Larson
Adapted from the episodes
"War of the Gods,
Parts I and II"
Written by Glen A. Larson

BERKLEY BOOKS, NEW YORK

BATTLESTAR GALACTICA 7:
WAR OF THE GODS

A Berkley Book / published by arrangement with
MCA PUBLISHING, a Division of MCA Communications, Inc.

PRINTING HISTORY
Berkley edition / December 1982

ISBN: 0-425-05660-0

A BERKLEY BOOK ® TM 757,375
Berkley Books are published by Berkley Publishing Corporation,
200 Madison Avenue, New York, New York 10016.
The name "BERKLEY" and the stylized "B" with design are
trademarks belonging to Berkley Publishing Corporation.
PRINTED IN THE UNITED STATES OF AMERICA

BattlestaR
GALACTICA 7
WAR OF THE GODS

There was once a time when humanity looked forward with great anticipation to first contact with alien races. No one truly believed that we were all alone. Somewhere out among the stars were other intelligent beings, possibly like us, possibly very different. What could they teach us? How much could we share? When the Twelve Colonies were first established, the descendents of the Lords of Kobol were all alone. We did not remain alone for long. We found other races, other beings. Some more advanced than we were, some more primitive. We welcomed contact with them all, envisioning a great universal brotherhood of species, a coming together of all life forms. Perhaps we were naive. Perhaps we were simply unrealistic. The Cylons changed all that.

It was almost a thousand yahrens before the date of my

birth that the Twelve Colonies and the Cylon Empire first made contact, a day that will live in infamy so long as one human remains alive. We held out our hands in friendship and the Cylons attacked with a savage, unrelenting fury. It was a long time before we were even able to discern the reason for their actions. By that time, the Twelve Colonies and the Cylon Empire were already engaged in a brutal war, one that was to be the longest and bloodiest in our history and one that was to end, perhaps forever, the glory that had sprung from the seeds sown by the Lords of Kobol eons ago. I have vowed that it will not happen, but time alone will tell. After all, I am just one man and my enemies are legion.

The reason for the war is so simple as to be incomprehensible. We were, according to the Cylons, unfit to engage in interstellar travel. Through some twisted sort of logic, they saw themselves as the guardians of the aesthetic order of the universe. It was their destiny to rule the stars, to regulate all inferior species—and, to Cylons, all species *were* inferior—and to eliminate any threat to what they perceived as the established order. The Colonies, of course, posed such a threat.

By the time that I was born, the war was already many yahrens old. It had become a fact of life to each and every man, woman and child in the Colonies. It is to the credit of the human race that we did not become a completely xenophobic people, but the word "alien" had taken on a whole new connotation. It was inextricably linked with certain base emotions—suspicion and distrust were chief among them. We were never again to encounter a new form of life without being on our guard. Survival was our prime consideration. We did not shoot first and ask questions later, but we had our guns out.

Sometimes, even that was not enough.

CHAPTER ONE

Four Viper fighters streaked across the void. The pilot of each ship was vibrantly alert. They kept in constant communication with each other to maintain their state of watchfulness. Their eyes seldom left their scanners as they scouted for any presence of the enemy. There was no room for error. Thousands upon thousands of lives depended on them. They each felt the keen responsibility that was theirs alone each time they went out on patrol. The welfare of the last surviving inhabitants of the twelve colony worlds was in their hands.

"This is Flight Leader to Advance Probe," said Bojay, speaking into the helmet mike that he could turn on and off with a quick flick of his tongue. "I think everything looks okay for the fleet in this sector. Let's start thinking about a last wide sweep and then heading for home. Copy?"

"Loud and clear," said Lieutenant Jolly. He was flying

point in the Viper formation, taking an advance scouting position well ahead of the other streamlined craft. "Making one final scanner sweep of—"

Without warning, the black void in front of Jolly's craft lit up with the radiance of several suns going nova. The pilot jerked back in his seat, involuntarily throwing his hands up in front of his face in an effort to shield himself from the searing glare.

"Bojay!"

The Flight Leader was receiving reports from every member of his patrol. They all spoke at once over the comcircuit.

"I'm seeing spots in front of my eyes . . . can't even make out the scanner. . . ."

"Never seen anything as bright as—"

"What in Kobol was—"

"All right, all right, put a lid on it," said Bojay, his own eyes smarting from the sting of the impossibly bright wash of light. "Take it easy, you guys. Whatever it was is gone now. Just hold steady on course till you can see straight again. Anybody injured?"

Negative reports came back over his helmet comcircuit.

"Okay. Let's check it out. We'll just ease over in that direction . . ."

"Maybe we'd better alert the fleet first," Jolly said.

"Let's just make certain what we're alerting them about," said Bojay. "There's plenty of time for—"

Another flash of light washed out the stars around them. Bojay heard Jolly's exclamation of pain and shock.

"Unnh! I not only saw that one, I *felt* it! What in the name of all that's holy could produce a flash like that?"

"Actuating automatic fleet alert," said Bojay. He still had no idea what was ahead of them, but he decided that it would be prudent to send a signal back to the *Galactica,* just in case whatever it was they would encounter would result in their failure to return. "Switching to long range scanners."

"Captain," said his wing man, "left center relative. . . ."

Bojay looked.

A swarm of bright pinpoint lights was approaching from the distance, moving with incredible speed. It was impossible to even estimate their number. They seemed to expand before their eyes as they hurtled toward them.

"I got 'em," Bojay said.

"Whatever they are, they're coming right at us and *fast,*" said Jolly.

"Actuate attack computers," Bojay said.

The pilots switched in their attack and defense systems. The scanners automatically locked on their target . . . except there was no target, according to the scanners. The turrets swept the area ahead of them, seeking a target to lock onto. The pilots had visual contact with whatever it was, but the scanners did not seem to be able to pick them up.

"Stand by to intercept," said Bojay.

"Captain," Jolly's voice came back to him over the com-circuit speakers built into his helmet, "I'm not picking them up on my scanner! *I'm not getting anything at all!*"

"Well, they're there, by God," said Bojay, setting his teeth. "And they're not slowing down."

The swarm of white lights grew rapidly. Each pilot found himself squinting, despite the polarization in both the shields of their helmets and the canopies of their Viper fighters. The glare was blindingly bright.

"Do we fire on them?" Jolly said.

"Not until we know if they're hostile," Bojay said, his

hands tightly gripping the controls of his ship.

"By the time we find that out . . ." Jolly did not complete the thought. Bojay knew exactly what was on the point man's mind. With the speed of the lights approaching them, it was doubtful if they would be able to fire with any degree of accuracy. Without the benefit of their scanners computing the rate of speed at which the swarm of lights traveled, it was impossible to lead them with their lasers.

Then there was no more time to think. The lights were upon them, streaking past the Vipers and crisscrossing, making a wide sweep around the fighter craft.

"Good Lord, they're fast!" said Bojay. "Anybody get a look at them?"

"No, sir," said Jolly. "It was all I could do to keep from closing my eyes. They're tearing up something fierce from all that glare. I'll tell you this, though, whatever they're flying, they can outrun us without even trying."

One of the other pilots was on the edge of panic. Bojay heard it in his voice.

"Let's get out of here! We've got to warn the fleet!"

"Hold your position," Bojay said sternly, trying to keep his voice calm. He could not afford to have any of his men lose their nerve. "I sent out an automatic alert already. Besides, so far we don't know if there's anything to warn them about. I repeat, hold your positions *and* your fire until we can figure out a way to get a fix on whatever that was. Anybody see anything?"

"No," said Jolly. "They just seem to have completely disappeared. I—no, wait. They're moving up behind us!"

No sooner had he spoken then the lights streaked past the Viper formation once again with such speed as to make the fighters appear to be motionless in space.

"Whatever the hell they are, they don't seem to be too interested in us," said Jolly. "Let's turn around and get out of here."

Bojay thought about the suggestion for a moment, then nodded to himself.

"Might as well," he said. "There doesn't seem to be anything more that we can do right now. Maybe the instruments on the *Galactica* can..."

His voice trailed off.

"Skipper?" Jolly said.

Bojay was speechless. He stared up at the mammoth ship that had appeared out of nowhere, flying directly above the Viper fighters, pacing them. It was huge, incredibly huge. Its bulk would have dwarfed even the *Galactica*.

"Skipper, my instruments are gone!" shouted the wing man. "I can't read a thing! What the hell *is* it?"

"Mine are spinning," Jolly said. "I'm caught in some sort of field, I can't control my ship! It feels like my head is going to burst, I can't stand it, the pressure..."

"What do we do?"

"Run for it," said Bojay. "Peel off and—"

"Bojay, I just lost power!" Jolly said, his voice filled with fear.

"Me, too, Skipper. Ship won't respond. I can't do a thing!"

Bojay heard one of the pilots screaming.

"My *head! God....*"

"Bojay!"

"I think we've just run up against something worse than Cylons," Bojay said, gritting his teeth against the pain. "We've had it, Jolly."

The pain became unbearable. Bojay stiffened in his seat,

holding onto his head, fighting to maintain consciousness. He couldn't do it. His eyes rolled up and he collapsed.

Starbuck and Apollo were both breathing heavily. They were in the final moment of a triad game. Above them, on all three sides of the triad court, the spectator stands were full of cheering onlookers.

The triad games were always very well attended. The fleet had precious few creature comforts, but recreation was one thing that could not be sacrificed. In a stress survival situation as demanding as theirs, in which attack from Cylons could come at any moment, in which the dull routine of daily duty could be interrupted, perhaps forever, by a searing blast of laser fire, it was necessary for there to be some way for people to unwind. One such mechanism could be found aboard the *Rising Star,* once an intercolonial starliner, now a ship that did double duty as a home for several thousand refugees and a gaming center, complete with casinos, entertainment lounges and sporting arenas. Here, people could forget, at least for a time, the rigors of their existence and spend a few precious centons gambling, enjoying a show put on by their fellow fleet members or playing any one of several sports that did not require a large amount of room. The most popular of these was the game called triad.

People had their favorite teams and their favorite players whom they supported with great enthusiasm. Those who did not or could not, for one reason or another, play themselves could easily experience the vicarious thrills of the sporting fan, cheering for their favorites and wagering on the outcome of the games. It was one of those activities in the fleet which had a great effect on the morale of the refugees.

The game was played by two teams of two. At the start of each period, it was determined by a flip of a cubit which team would start off defending and which attacking. A member of each team stood face-to-face in the center of the court. Behind the defending team, against one of the walls, would be a ball approximately the size of a human head. It was made of a hard, polymesh nysteel compound, which gave it peculiar bouncing properties and at the same time added an element of danger to the game, since being hit by the ball could easily result in serious injury. To minimize the chances of being hurt, the players all wore light nysteel helmets and polymesh gloves. Other protective gear, which was optional, consisted of a polymesh vest that covered the chest area and dropped down to protect the groin, leaving the hips exposed, and flexible boots that protected the shins and knees. The soles of the boots were molded from impact resistant velotex, a material which had strong adhesive properties, enabling the players to "climb the walls" of the triad court, although they could not, in the strictest sense, cling to the smooth surfaces for more than a fraction of a micron.

The two forward team members of each team who stood at center court at the start of each period had a line between them. When the claxon sounded to announce the start of the period, the offensive player had to physically move past the forward defender to get the ball. The defending player could not cross the line in front of him, nor could he move behind a line that was several feet behind him, between him and the ball. In effect, he had to prevent the offensive player from crossing a narrow corridor he was protecting. How-

ever, there were few rules specifying what the defending
player could or could not do to prevent the offensive player
from getting by him. This frequently gave the start of each
period of play an aspect of the martial arts. In this sense,
it was much more than a simple competitive sport. It gave
the players, most of whom were warriors in the championship league, a way of keeping in top fighting trim. There
was no limit of time to determine how long the offensive
player had to get by the defender to put the ball in play,
although there was a definite time limit to each period.
Theoretically, it was possible for entire periods to be devoted
entirely to sporting combat between two forwards only,
since the two remaining players could not get into the game
until the ball was put into play.

Once the ball was put into play, however, the triad game
began in earnest, and it was played at a fast and furious
level. Once the offensive player picked up the ball, he could
aim it at any of three lighted circles that appeared on any
and all three walls. These circles flashed on and off at
random, the sequence controlled by a computer, and a circle
had to be struck while it was lighted to result in a score.
The circles, when lighted, bore numbers which also were
controlled in random sequence, each number carrying a
point value from one to ten. The higher the number, the
more difficult the target, since the higher numbered circles
were illuminated for a shorter length of time than those
which had lower point values.

The defending players had to attempt to anticipate the
play of the offensive team, so that they could cover a target
circle and either deflect the ball or regain control of it, in
which case they became the offensive team. Passing was
permitted in the game, but only if the ball was rebounded

off one of the walls. An interception gave a defender offensive status and the next scoring opportunity.

Starbuck and Apollo were both sweating, the result of their exertions in what had thus far been a fairly evenly matched game against Boomer and Greenbean. The galleries were going wild in full appreciation of a fast, closely matched bout.

Starbuck and Boomer squared off against each other in center court to begin the final period of play. The claxon sounded and Starbuck instantly executed a lightning fast double roundhouse kick, alternately striking first at Boomer's left temple, then his right. Boomer blocked the first kick with his forearm, but Starbuck scored a hit with his second kick, striking Boomer's helmet just above his temple. Boomer grunted and staggered for a moment, during which time Starbuck attempted to bolt past him. As he drew level with Boomer, the latter executed a foot sweep and Starbuck went down to the floor of the court like a ton of bricks. They were now both in the defensive corridor. Apollo and Greenbean watched anxiously from the rear of each side of the court, each man ready to dart instantly to either side the moment that the ball was touched. Until that time, neither man was allowed to move.

Boomer dived down on Starbuck in an attempt to sit on him and pin him, prone, to the floor, but Starbuck rolled to one side and regained his feet. Both men stood up, breathing heavily, each watching for an opportunity to make a strike. The fans were screaming, exhorting them to combat.

Starbuck kept moving from side to side, trying to fake Boomer out so that he could dash by him, but Boomer responded to his every move, interposing his body between Starbuck and the ball. Starbuck feinted a forward lunge, then used his momentum to spin around. While he was spinning, he brought his rear leg around in a vicious arc, using the momentum of his spin to impart force to the wheel kick. His heel caught Boomer in the side, just above his kidney. Had not Boomer been wearing his protective polymesh vest, the force of the strike could well have crippled him. As it was, he was stunned and Starbuck rushed by him, running to the far wall to pick up the ball. The moment that he touched the ball, triad was in session.

The audience supporting his team broke into a spontaneous chant.

"*Star*-buck, *Star*-buck, *Star*-buck, *Star*-buck. . . ."

Starbuck picked up the ball. Boomer and Greenbean were both in motion, Boomer moving toward Starbuck in an attempt to block a scoring throw or a pass to Apollo, Greenbean moving to cover Apollo, trying to stay with him as Apollo attempted to fake him out and get clear for a pass.

Starbuck feinted with a scoring throw at the ten circle, and as Boomer leapt up to block the shot, Starbuck turned quickly and rammed the ball into the wall to his immediate right. The ball caroomed off the wall, the angle of the rebound causing it to pass behind Greenbean and into Apollo's outstretched hands.

The loud slap of the ball against Apollo's protective gloves reverberated throughout the court.

Apollo cocked his arm to throw at the five circle opposite him, but instead threw the ball back to Starbuck, bouncing it off the wall to his left. The ball hit the wall and rebounded at a geometrically impossible angle, its wild flight due to the unstable properties of polymesh nysteel. Starbuck failed to anticipate the ball's flightpath and it passed him, to bounce off the third wall. Boomer spun to catch the rebound, but the ball came back high and, as Boomer flexed his legs to make a leap for it, Starbuck ran two steps forward and "climbed" Boomer's back, stepping between his shoulder blades and launching himself upward to catch the ball. It slapped into his gloves and before he could touch down again, Starbuck turned in midair like a highdiver and hurled the ball at a ten circle. It struck microns before the circle winked out and a bell sounded, announcing the score. Almost at the same time, the claxon rang out, ending the final period and the game. Starbuck and Apollo won by a narrow margin of ten points.

The two players were almost instantly mobbed by their fans, who jumped down out of the galleries and onto the court, thronging around their favorites in spite of all efforts of the security personnel to hold them back.

"Off the court, off the court," the head security guard kept shouting, to no avail. "Come on, people, this is strictly forbidden. Let's get these guys out of here."

Athena pushed through the guards and rushed up to Starbuck and her brother. Sheba came through right behind her.

"You were incredible tonight, incredible," Athena said, grinning widely.

"We got some lucky boards," Apollo said.

Starbuck laughed. "Speak for yourself, partner. I was brilliant."

"I'll second that," Athena said. "Now what can I do to reward you for your excellence?" The look she gave Starbuck was outrageously flirtatious.

"Give me a few centons to change," he said. "I'm sure I'll be able to think of something."

They linked arms and moved off the court together as the security guards tried to make a path for them. Hands kept reaching out and slapping Starbuck on the back.

"Well," said Sheba to Apollo, "I don't know if I'd go so far as to say you were incredible, but I might be able to grant that you were reasonably proficient and buy you a drink."

"Generous, very generous," said Apollo. "You've got a deal. I'll meet you in the Officer's Club back aboard the *Galactica*."

Sheba turned and pushed back through the crowd as Apollo turned to Boomer, who was still a bit groggy from having been forced to the ground by Starbuck's use of him as a stepladder.

"Nice play, Boomer," said Apollo.

"Yeah, sure," mumbled Boomer morosely. "Just once, I'd like to beat you two. Just once."

"Don't worry about it, Boomer. I'm sure there's something you're good at." Apollo grinned.

"For *that*, you're buying," Boomer said, laughing. "You're starting to sound too much like Starbuck for my tastes."

As the security guards struggled to keep the crowd under control, Tigh broke through the press.

"I'm afraid nobody's buying," he said tersely. "Emergency meeting in the War Room."

"Hey, Tigh," said Apollo, "we're not even on standby."

"Yeah, have a heart, Colonel," Boomer added, "we've just run ourselves ragged playing triad. I *need* a drink."

"You may need one even more when you find out what's happened," Tigh said.

They wasted no time in changing and getting back aboard the shuttle that would take them to the *Galactica*. Once on the shuttle, they started pumping Tigh for information concerning what had happened. They didn't like what they heard at all.

The mood in the War Room of the *Battlestar Galactica* was a somber one. Adama, Tigh, Starbuck, Apollo, Sheba and Boomer stood before the star map.

"They disappeared here," said Adama, pointing to the map, "in this sector."

"No transmissions of any kind?" said Apollo.

Tigh and Adama exchanged looks.

"We received the automatic fleet distress signal," Tigh said.

"Since then," said Adama, "nothing. Four Viper fighters have simply vanished."

Apollo licked his lips nervously and moved up to the map.

"What about here? What kind of land mass is indicated?"

Adama moved to the scanner, checking computer readings and information tapes.

"We don't know," he said after a moment, shaking his head. "However, seismic readings indicate something has happened there within a time frame that could have a bearing on our missing ships. I realize I'm imposing on your rest period, but—"

"You don't have to say it, Commander," Sheba said. "Bojay is like family to me. He's all that's left from . . ."

Her voice trailed off. She didn't have to finish the sentence. They all knew what she was talking about, what must have been going through her mind. Bojay was the only other person aboard the *Galactica* who served with Sheba on the *Pegasus*, the scarred battlestar commanded by her father, Cain. The Juggernaut. And no one knew if he was dead or alive. Bojay was her only link to the past. They had flown together in the same squadron. The Silver Spar squadron now made its base aboard the *Battlestar Galactica*, but none of the original members was left.

"I'll get my gear," said Sheba.

Apollo watched her leave, striding purposefully out of the War Room.

"Maybe sending her is a mistake," he said softly. "There's been no trace of her father or the *Pegasus* since his disappearance. Now, losing Bojay . . ."

Starbuck shook his head.

"I disagree that emotion could be a factor in finding those four pilots," he said. "We're all equally affected and equally motivated. Jolly is like a brother to me."

Apollo glanced at his father.

"I guess we've got the right team, then," he said.

"Apollo," Adama said, "don't take any chances. If they're not on that planet, then . . ."

Apollo nodded grimly. "I know. They wouldn't have had fuel enough to have been in continuous flight since they left. If we don't find them, we'll come right back."

They both pivoted smart about-faces and left the room together. Adama watched Starbuck and Apollo as they left, thinking how much they both reminded him of the way he had been when he was young. He hoped fervently that they would both have a chance to feel that way about their sons someday.

"Commander," said Tigh, "that seismic reading . . . I don't like the implications of it. It's too sudden and abortive to be a core tremor. More likely, it was an explosion of some kind."

"But it's hardly likely that four Viper fighters crashed simultaneously," said Adama.

"No, but they could have been on the ground when whatever it was hit."

Adama took a deep breath and let it out slowly.

"Let's withhold speculation for a while," he said. "We'll know soon enough."

CHAPTER TWO

They drew lots to determine who would remain behind as backup in case they had to send for another Viper in a hurry. Standard operating procedure dictated that any rescue recon mission in which the probability of there being no survivors was high could number no more than three Viper fighters. It was, perhaps, a harsh regulation, but then in a situation where the fleet could come under attack at almost any time, it was necessary to conserve their fighting strength as much as possible. Besides, they could not afford to lose Vipers. Boomer lost the draw.

Starbuck, Apollo and Sheba suited up and entered the cockpits of their Viper fighters, went through their pre-flight checks and waited for the word to launch. It came from Tigh over their helmet comcircuits.

They kicked in their turbos and hurtled down the launch tubes. As always, there was that sudden pressure against their chests as they were slammed back against their seats, as if held there by a giant hand. Then, there was the magical sensation that no one ever really got over, the wonder of that first moment in which the fighter ship cleared the launch tubes and hurtled into the deep velvet dark of space.

They formed into triangle formation as they set course to match that taken by the lost recon patrol. Each of them was alone with their own thoughts. It could have been any one of them. There was no telling what had happened. They could have run into some freak cosmic storm. They could have blundered into a Cylon patrol. There was an infinite number of possibilities.

The planet loomed before them.

"What do you think?" said Starbuck, anxious to break the tense, unaccustomed silence.

"Tell you in a flash," Apollo said. He punched up his scanner. A grim reading confronted him.

"NO LIFE FORMS . . . NO LIFE FORMS . . . NO LIFE FORMS . . ."

"You got it?" said Apollo.

"Yeah," said Starbuck, seeing the same reading flash across his own ship's scanner. He sounded suddenly weary.

"I wonder why no life forms," Sheba's voice came over their comcircuit. "The planet seems to have the appropriate atmospheric conditions."

"It's possible that no travelers from the Colonies ever made it out this far," Apollo said.

"At least if they did, they didn't hang around for some reason," Starbuck said.

"That doesn't bode well for the direction we're heading in to find the lost thirteenth tribe," said Sheba.

"One problem at a time," Apollo said. "Let's take 'em down."

The three Vipers angled down toward the pale red planet and entered its atmosphere. Their engines roared like angry beasts as the ships skimmed low over the planet's surface.

"Starbuck...Apollo...look at the color of the vegetation," Sheba said. "It's all red."

"Maybe it's all dead," Starbuck said.

"Let's find a place to set down and have a look," said Apollo.

"There!" said Starbuck. "Just over that rise. Take a look at that."

It was an incredibly large area that had been completely burned out.

"Looks like something big hit here," said Apollo.

"I got it on visual," said Starbuck. "Just to the left of center. Some kind of wreckage. Kobol, whatever it was must have been *huge*."

"Let's swing around and go in," Apollo said.

The Vipers banked and came around once more. Like giant birds sweeping in for a landing, they set down on the soft red grass just beyond the crest of the crater.

Apollo was the first to pop up his canopy and drop to the ground. He quickly surveyed the area. Behind him, a short distance away, Starbuck was climbing out of his ship. Sheba was already running toward him across the grassy red meadow. They gathered together beside Apollo's ship.

"There's something very strange about this place," said Starbuck. "What's that smell?"

"I don't know," Apollo said. "I've never smelled anything like it. But it has a pungent, decaying sort of flavor."

He made a face. "It isn't very pleasant, whatever it is."

Starbuck plucked some grass up from between his feet. He rubbed the blades with his fingers, then smelled them.

"This is what it is," he said. "But this stuff isn't dead."

"And that's not all that's alive," said Apollo.

Starbuck and Sheba saw that he was staring off into the distance, at the crest of the crater. They followed his gaze.

A lone figure stood at the crest of the hill, strangely backlighted. His cloak billowed in the breeze. The wind seemed to gain strength and a bolt of lightning stabbed down from the blood red sky.

"I thought the scanners read no life forms," said Starbuck.

"Obviously an erroneous reading," Apollo said, although he didn't sound quite sure of himself.

As they watched, the man standing on the ridge turned and disappeared into the crater.

"Whoever he is, he doesn't want to talk," Apollo said. "Let's see why."

All three took off up the hill toward the ridge at a dead run. They were slightly winded when they reached the crest. Their expressions showed their confusion.

Before them, in the crater, was a blackened area devoid of any signs of life. In the center of the crater were the skeletal remains of a mammoth ship that had crashed and burned.

"Where did he go?" said Sheba.

"That's a very good question," said Apollo.

"*Damn*. Look at that thing," said Starbuck. "I thought it looked huge from the air, but this. . . ."

Apollo unstrapped his portable scanner from his leg.

"Let's go down and have a look," he said.

They started down the hill.

"I wouldn't go down there," said a voice from behind them.

They spun around, startled.

An incredible vision confronted them. Standing on the crest of the crater, where they had stood only microns ago, was the man they had seen earlier. He was of slightly above average height and he appeared to be human. His face had a chiseled, patrician look about it and his hair was black and swept back from his forehead. He had a regal bearing, all the more accentuated by his amazing apparel. He was dressed in robes made of a white, velvety material with a collar that stood high above his head. He made no move toward them, merely stood still and composed on the top of the ridge.

"The radion levels are extremely high down there," he said.

Apollo stared at him. "Where in Kobol did you come from?"

"Where did *you* come from?" countered the man, raising his eyebrows.

The three warriors exchanged uncertain looks.

"What is this place?" said Starbuck. "And who are you?"

"Who are *you?*" the man countered again.

"Look," said Apollo, "this game isn't getting us any-place."

"Ah, but I was here first," said the man. His voice seemed to hold a slightly mocking edge.

"We mean you no harm," Apollo said. "We're friends. You're obviously human. If you want our help, we're more than ready to assist you."

"It's more likely that *I* can help *you,*" the man said.

"How?" said Starbuck. "Are there others like you?"

"Not here," came the reply.

"But in some other place?"

"Many!"

Apollo and Starbuck glanced at each other and saw that each of them was thinking that the man could very likely be unbalanced.

"That ship..." said Sheba, pointing at the burned-out hulk that dwarfed them all.

"Yes."

"How did it crash?"

"It was destroyed," he said.

"By whom?" said Apollo.

"The great powers," the man replied cryptically.

"Do you mean the Cylon Empire?" said Sheba.

"No."

"Then just who are these powers?" Sheba persisted.

"It's difficult to explain," the stranger said. "Can we move away from here? I don't want to be reminded of what happened to my people."

He turned and started walking down the hill, in the direction of their ships. Apollo glanced down at his scanner. He tapped it slightly with his hand.

"What is it?" said Starbuck.

"He doesn't give off a reading," Apollo said. "No brain waves, no pulse, nothing."

Starbuck gave Apollo a wry look, then unstrapped his own scanner and aimed it toward the departing man. The stranger was almost out of sight behind the ridge. He stopped in his tracks and spoke to them without looking back.

"You won't find your scanners to be of much use," he

said. "The radion field here from the crash is much too strong. It causes interference."

He disappeared behind the ridge.

They climbed back to the crest again. For a moment, they couldn't see him, then they spotted him, sitting down in a veritable oasis in the middle of the plain. It was astonishing that none of them had spotted it before. There was a small brook, a few large rocks surrounded by shrubs and small trees.

"Who *is* this guy?" said Starbuck out of the corner of his mouth.

"I don't know," said Apollo. "But I somehow have the feeling that we've stumbled onto something that could change our lives."

Starbuck looked at his friend with amazement.

"Change our lives? What are you talking about? He's just one guy!"

"Just one man," Apollo nodded. "Who gives off an incredibly commanding aura. And who claims to have survived that fiery crash without a mark on him."

"I feel weary," the stranger said. "Drained of my strength."

Sheba knelt down beside him. She dipped her hand into the water and bathed his forehead.

"We have emergency rations with us," she said. "We'll gladly share them with you."

"How kind of you," he said. "But no, it is not food that I require."

"How did you survive that crash?" Apollo said.

The stranger did not look at him. His eyes were focused on something in the distance.

"I don't know," he said.

"You spoke of your people," Starbuck said. "They were on that ship?"

The stranger nodded. "Yes. They are all gone. What about you? Your people? You will be returning to them soon?"

"Yes," said Apollo.

"I wonder if I might accompany you," the stranger said.

"I'd like to know a little more about you," said Apollo. "Who you are, where you come from. . . ."

"You do not know my people," said the stranger. "They are not from your world."

"But if they are human, there must be a connection," Starbuck said hopefully. "Maybe—"

"Maybe," said the stranger. "Maybe I can help you in your quest."

"What quest was that?" Apollo said.

"Whatever you are looking for," the man in white replied. "My knowledge of the universe is infinite. I think we should be going."

He stood abruptly and moved off toward their ships.

"Likeable," said Starbuck, "but a bit on the loony side if you ask me."

"Maybe," said Apollo. "Maybe not. I want to know where he came from."

"You keep saying that," said Sheba. "What difference does it make? He's human. And he's all alone."

Apollo looked at Sheba and frowned.

"Sheba, why are you suddenly so protective of him? So far, he's been nothing but evasive with us."

"He's probably just confused," she said, "disoriented. Maybe he's still in shock from the explosion."

"That would make sense," said Starbuck. "If he ejected from that ship, he would have taken a bad fall."

"Doesn't look too banged up to me," Apollo said.

"Well," said Starbuck, shrugging his shoulders, "we can't very well leave him behind."

"Have you considered that he might be some sort of spy?" Apollo said. "He might have been planted here."

"Who knew we were coming?" Starbuck said.

"Whoever was responsible for our patrol disappearing."

Starbuck considered it.

"He's only one man," he said. "If we keep our guard up, I don't see what he could do."

"Let's just make sure he isn't carrying any kind of homing device," said Apollo.

"Good idea," Sheba said. "If this is one more of Baltar's little tricks, maybe it'll backfire."

They caught up to the man.

"We've decided to take you with us," said Apollo.

The stranger only smiled.

"Starbuck, go back to the ship and tell them to send a shuttle," said Apollo. "And see if there's been any word of the missing patrol," he added, although he wasn't optimistic.

Starbuck jumped into his Viper and was airborne in a flash. As he streaked off into space, there was the sudden sound of several explosions in the distance and the red sky washed out to white on the horizon. White balls of light, impossibly bright, streaked across the sky toward them at astonishing speeds. It did not seem possible to the warriors that anything could move that fast, yet the white balls of searing light hurtled across the sky so quickly that they almost hurt their necks trying to follow their progress. They emitted a piercing high-pitched sound that became deafening the closer they came and as they passed by overhead, both warriors doubled over and clutched at their heads, covering their ears in an effort to block out the nerve-shattering noise. The stranger, however, stood straight and tall, staring at the balls of light with what looked like defiance. There was a look of cold fury in his eyes. They seemed to blaze with an unholy light.

"What *is* it?" moaned Sheba. "What's happening?"

"It didn't even faze him," said Apollo, rubbing his temples to assuage the sudden headache caused by the sound of the white objects.

"We'd better hurry," said the stranger. "They'll come back. They're looking for me."

"One more thing before we go," said Apollo. "You say that we wouldn't know of your world, but that your knowledge of the universe is infinite. Have you ever heard of a planet called Earth?"

"I have been there," said the stranger.

The warriors glanced at each other with astonishment.

"Then you know where it is!" said Sheba.

"Yes."

The three Vipers escorted the shuttle from the *Galactica* back to the ship. As they neared the battlestar, the ships went into an approach pattern. As each ship contacted the invisible force field of the landing bay, the black box wired into its guidance system cancelled out the field so that the craft could pass through the atmospheric shield as if through a semi-permeable membrane. There was a popping sound that accompanied the passage of each ship through the field as some of the atmosphere inside the ship escaped into space, but the amount lost was infinitessimal and did not inconvenience the ground crews who worked in the landing bay.

The ships lined up on their landing points and settled slowly to the deck of the landing bay. The ground crews rushed forward to secure the craft and to begin their maintenance tasks.

Colonel Tigh moved hurriedly toward the ships. Apollo popped his cockpit, as did Starbuck. Tigh quickly moved to them.

"Any sign of the others?" he said anxiously.

"No," Apollo said, his voice heavy with regret. "We came up empty. Well, not quite."

Apollo nodded his head toward the shuttle. The stranger in white was stepping down onto the landing bay deck. Sheba walked up to him and together they approached Colonel Tigh.

"May I introduce our guest, Count Iblis?" Sheba said. "Colonel Tigh," she said. "And this is Athena." She indicated Apollo's sister, who had also come down to meet the recon rescue party.

"A great honor, Colonel," said Count Iblis. "I know that your mind must be filled with questions at this moment, but I wonder if I might first find a place to rest from my ordeal?"

"I'll be glad to give you and my father a quick debriefing," Apollo said to Tigh, "but I'm sure he'll eventually want to talk to Count Iblis at length."

"Of course," said Tigh. "Sheba, after you've all been through de-con, proceed to the life station, then find the count some quarters."

Sheba and the count both moved off in the direction of the de-con section.

"I'll see you two immediately after you've finished here," said Tigh to Starbuck and Apollo.

As soon as they went through the standard post-mission decontamination procedures, Apollo and Starbuck hurried to Commander Adama's quarters with Colonel Tigh. Adama was waiting for them in his cabin, pacing nervously. He beckoned all three men to their seats impatiently.

"All right," he said. "I want to hear about this Count Iblis. You say he was all alone on this planet?"

"Alone, beside the wreckage of an immense ship of unfamiliar design," Apollo said.

"Did you investigate the wreckage?" Adama said.

"No, sir," said Starbuck. "It was giving off exceptionally high radion levels. There was interference with our scanners. We couldn't move into the area without returning to the *Galactica* for special gear."

"Yet Count Iblis survived," said Adama, "despite the radion levels?"

"I can only speculate that he must have ejected from the ship before it crashed," Apollo said. "We didn't see any evidence of an ejection pod, but he could have jettisoned himself from the ship when it was struck and landed quite some distance away, then traveled overland to the wreckage site."

"You said the ship was struck," Adama said. "By whom? Cylons?"

"Not according to Count Iblis," Starbuck said. "But then there's no telling what condition his mind might be in after an encounter such as he's been through."

"All right," said Adama. "I want a complete report on Count Iblis from the life station. Cranial probe, neuro systems, everything up to and including psychoelectron recall."

"Don't you think that some sort of, well, formal greeting might be in order before we ask him to submit to all that?" Apollo said.

"Yes, yes, of course," said Adama. "Bring him up to my quarters as soon as possible. Give him as much time as he needs to rest and as soon as he feels up to talking, I'd like to see him."

"Father?" said Apollo.

"Yes, is there something else?"

"I don't know. It might just be incoherent rambling, dissociation as a result of shock, maybe he was simply trying to find a way to convince us to take him along, but he said he's been to Earth."

Adama's eyes grew wide.

"He said *what?*"

"That he's been to Earth. That he knows where it is."

Adama licked his lips nervously.

"You are to say nothing of this to anyone, is that understood?" he said. "I don't want to start any rumors flying around this ship. It could be as you suppose, that he just said that to induce you to bring him back to the *Galactica*. If it's really true . . ." Adama shook his head. "I don't even want to speculate about that now. I'm afraid to raise my own hopes. But I am very, very anxious to speak to this Count Iblis. Very anxious, indeed."

Sheba and Count Iblis walked down the corridor leading to the life station. Iblis glanced about casually, as if only mildly interested in his new surroundings.

"We can stop here for some hypernutrients and a quick energon treatment," Sheba said. "It will get your strength up and get you through the debriefing."

"No," said Iblis.

He stopped dead in his tracks. Sheba was taken aback. She kept walking past him for several steps before realizing he had stopped. She turned and stared at him quizzically.

"It's not that I don't appreciate your concern," said Count Iblis in a placating tone. He smiled at her charmingly. "It's just that I have concerns of my own."

"We only want to help you," Sheba said.

"I'm sure," said Iblis, "but you don't understand. I don't come from your world. Or from your time. I must consider the possibility that your instruments could well prove to be destructive to me."

"They're the very latest—" Sheba began, but Iblis cut her off.

"For your time, yes. Actually, your ships . . . your wonderful developments . . . all are quite admirable. However, your systems are . . . *different.*"

He smiled at her again. It was such an honest, open and engaging smile that any objections Sheba might have had to his protestations simply evaporated.

"I would very much like to see more of your ship, if I may," said Count Iblis.

"I really should be getting you to . . ." Sheba stopped. Iblis was looking at her and smiling. And she couldn't tear her eyes away from his. She seemed to be falling into them. Something in his pupils seemed to blaze.

"What do you mean he never went to the life station?" said Adama. "Just where *is* he?"

Tigh shook his head helplessly. "I'll find him immediately," he said.

Count Iblis was on the bridge of the *Galactica*, with Sheba by his side. She was smiling and pointing out to him the controls of the ship, the various systems, explaining their functions.

"This is the communication center," she said, indicating Athena's console. "With this system, we maintain a constant monitor on all of the ships in our fleet."

As Iblis approached the screen, the monitor began to break up into static and snow. Athena frowned and tried to adjust the controls, but nothing seemed to work. Something was causing massive interference.

"I'm sorry," she said, puzzled. "We seem to be having a problem with some sort of electrical interference. It was fine just a micron ago."

"One of the problems of space travel," explained Sheba. "Electrical fields, equipment failures, I'm sure you understand."

"Completely," said Count Iblis.

As they moved on to another area of the bridge, Athena's scanner monitors cleared up. She simply shrugged and dismissed it.

Tigh entered Adama's quarters. The commander was seated at his table, enjoying a relaxing beverage. It wasn't doing much to relax him. He drummed his fingers nervously on the surface of the table.

"I just received word from the bridge," said Colonel Tigh. "Our visitor just left there with Sheba. We're tracking them down now."

"Tracking them down?" said Adama. "Colonel, what are we running here? A perfect stranger comes aboard the *Galactica* and he's being shown sensitive military control centers without so much as a hello, who are you?"

"It does seem a little out of the ordinary," said Tigh weakly.

"Out of the ordinary?"

Tigh winced. When Adama grew angry, heads rolled.

"I don't know what possessed Sheba to do it," he said. "I'll find them both and have them here in microns."

"That would be very nice," said Adama. "On the other hand, perhaps you shouldn't bother. The way things seem to be going, no doubt Count Iblis will soon be getting a guided tour of this very room."

Tigh gritted his teeth. "I'll find them right away, Commander."

"See that you do."

"The rejuvenation center is this way," said Sheba as they walked down the corridor together. Iblis was taking it all in. "It might be a good place for you to stop and rest for a while. We've covered a lot of ground."

Count Iblis stopped. His eyes seemed to unfocus for a moment.

"No," he said. "It's time to find Commander Adama."

"You know Commander Adama?" Sheba said. She did not recall anyone mentioning the commander's name in his presence.

"Someone must have mentioned his name on the bridge," said Count Iblis with a smile. "Was I incorrect? Is he not your leader?"

There was something about his look and smile that was

so disarming that Sheba immediately relaxed.

"Oh, he's our leader, all right," she said. "This way, I'll take you to his quarters."

At that moment, Adama was pacing in his quarters, his anger and frustration growing. It was absurd. A man no one knew, from who knows where, was wandering about the ship and no one could seem to find him. What in the name of Kobol was going on? Had security completely broken down?

"Just where in the name of Hades *is* he," Adama said, his voice tense with barely controlled fury. "How did he get free run of this ship? Now which of you has an answer for me?"

He glared at Starbuck and Apollo. The two pilots were clearly ill at ease.

"Uh, well . . ." Apollo stammered, not having the faintest idea of how to explain to his father what had happened, since he didn't understand it himself.

"Well, the last we saw of him," Starbuck began, but at that moment Count Iblis entered the room with Sheba.

"Pardon me," he said.

So surprised were they at his sudden entrance that no one noticed Adama's monitor screens going haywire as Iblis passed them. The moment he walked by the console, the screens returned to normal.

"You are Commander Adama," Count Iblis said, his voice full of respect. "Count Iblis, at your service."

He approached the commander of the battlestar and went down on one knee and bowed his head slightly. Adama stared at him, completely taken aback.

"I'll want to talk to each of you later," he said to Starbuck and Apollo. "You'll be notified. In the meantime, I'd like a few centons alone with Count Iblis."

"Yes, sir," both pilots said in unison. And, grateful that Iblis' timely arrival had spared them a tongue lashing by Adama, they quickly withdrew.

"Be in one place," Adama said as they were leaving. They paused. "I wouldn't want to have to search all over the ship for *you*."

The pilots stiffened.

"Would the Officer's Club be suitable?" said Starbuck.

"Predictable would be a better choice of words," Adama said wryly, "but yes, fine. See that you stay there."

"Yes, sir."

"Good. Dismissed, gentlemen."

They wasted no time in leaving.

In the corridor, both men sighed with relief. Starbuck glanced at Apollo and whistled softly.

"Man, I don't think I've ever seen him so unsettled."

"You'd think we just deserted him or something," Sheba said. She had left with them. Adama had said nothing to her, but the look that he had given her spoke volumes.

"It is a little difficult to understand why you took a perfect stranger into classified areas," Apollo said.

"He asked me to," said Sheba.

"You do everything you're asked to do?"

"Apollo!"

"You know what I mean."

"Look," she said, "I'll admit that it looks a little awkward and it's kind of hard to explain, but . . . it wasn't what he said as much as what I felt. He needed to feel that there was order and security. So I took him where I thought the environment would help to settle him down. It worked. He's feeling much better now."

Apollo stared at her for a moment. Something simply did not make sense. He felt that he was missing something.

"You've been acting like this ever since we found the count," he said. "Or he found us. What makes him so important to you? You don't even know who he is! None of us do!"

"I know that he cares," said Sheba.

"For you?"

"For all of us. And if I have to explain it to you, you're less sensitive than I thought."

She walked away from them, obviously annoyed. Apollo shook his head in bewilderment.

"She thinks I'm insensitive," he said, trying to run it through again and make some sort of sense out of it. He wasn't succeeding.

"You?" said Starbuck. "If she thinks *you're* insensitive, where does that leave me?"

Adama was sitting behind his desk, his elbows on the desktop, hands clasped before his chin. He watched Count Iblis intently. The stranger was seated across the room, before the observation port.

"I am eternally grateful to you for delivering me from my enemies," said Count Iblis.

"Tell me about your enemies," Adama said.

"They are infinite," Iblis replied. "They are everywhere. And they are relentless."

Adama nodded. "I know a little about that kind of enemy myself," he said. "But their name. . . . What are they called? Where are they from?"

The look on Count Iblis' face was cold. He seemed to seethe with internal fire.

"Forgive my passion," he said, "my inability to communicate with you. But there are things which you might not understand."

"You'd be surprised, Count Iblis," said Adama. "I'm quite a bright fella when given a chance."

Iblis smiled.

"Yes, of course. Forgive me. Of course you are. And generous, too, to stop for one more survivor. Precisely why I am not sure that it would be wise to burden you with my fight."

"I don't mean to suggest that we can take on any more enemies than we already have," Adama said, "but perhaps we are already fighting a common foe."

"There are great and infinitely more dangerous powers in the universe than your Cylons," Iblis said. "And all their allies combined."

The expression on Adama's face was grave as he considered the import of Iblis' words.

"You see?" said Count Iblis. "Already I have alarmed you. Now allow me to bring you a more optimistic piece of news. You are searching for a place called Earth."

"My son told you that?" said Adama.

"Not exactly," Iblis replied, "but you are of the House of Kobol. Your tribes are scattered. The thirteenth journeyed to Earth several millenniums ago."

"Then they *are* there," said Adama, leaning forward. "Tell me about their civilization."

"It has known great rises and falls," said Iblis.

"And now?" Adama said. "Now they are strong? Can they help us in our fight against the Cylon Empire?"

"Your people will be safe under my leadership."

Adama frowned. "Did I understand you correctly? Did

you say under *your* leadership?"

"Of course, Adama. Why do you think I am here? I have come to prepare your way to Earth."

FROM THE ADAMA JOURNALS:

Despite all precautions, word of the mysterious stranger who calls himself Count Iblis has swept throughout the fleet. His promises are giving our people the first real hope they've had in a quarter yahren. Still, his presence, his unwillingness to submit to routine medical procedures leaves me with grave doubts about the integrity of his mind or his ability to deliver on his promises.

One more disappointment in the lives of our poor, beleaguered survivors might spell the end of our journey or my ability to maintain order. Still, the possibility of hope cannot be dismissed lightly.

Many questions still remain. Who *is* Count Iblis, if that is truly his name? *What* is he? He seems, to all external appearances, to be human, as are we, yet how is it possible for one human being to possess infinite knowledge of the universe, as he claims? Where is he from? What is the nature of the enemy that pursues him? Who are they? What is the basis of their conflict? Iblis remains a puzzle, a strange enigma.

On the one hand, it would seem a fairly simple matter to insist that my questions be answered. I could demand that he submit to examination, that he cease giving evasive, enigmatic answers to all my queries. I *could* force him. Yet, that possibility brings up yet another question.

What if his claims are not exaggerated? What if he really can deliver what he promises?

If Iblis can, indeed, bring us to Earth, it would be the answer to all our prayers. We have been searching, blindly, following an ancient trail, not even sure that our path is the correct one. Do I have the right to risk the future of every man, woman and child in the fleet simply because I have my doubts about Count Iblis? Have all these yahrens of fighting made me overly distrustful and suspicious?

I must also consider the fact that Count Iblis could be suspicious of us. He claims to be from another world, from another time. From his words, it would seem that he is from a culture far in advance of ours. Would not such a culture suspect barbarian primitives, as we would seem to them? He has told me that the fleet would be safe under his leadership. Part of me regards that as an arrogant threat, yet another part of me admits another, much more astonishing possibility.

Count Iblis says that he knows where Earth is, that he has been there. Suppose, just suppose, that Count Iblis *is from Earth*. Could it not be possible, if their culture is so far ahead of ours, that they would have some means of probing across vast distances of space, of learning of our presence? Could they not possess ships vastly superior to our own?

What if they sent Count Iblis ahead as an advance scout, to feel us out, to find out what our intentions were, what sort of people we are? We never did find any trace of the recon patrol commanded by Bojay. There is, of course, the sad possibility that they have met their fate. There is an even more incredible possibility, that they were captured by a ship from Earth, that they are being studied at this very moment. . . .

What am I saying? I'm becoming carried away by wild flights of fancy. But it *could* be possible. I cannot dismiss even the wildest speculation in this case.

If Iblis were to be examined, it would prove conclusively if he were of our kind. But Iblis will not allow it. And I cannot insist. At this point, I dare not. Never before has the weight of my responsibility lain as heavily on my shoulders. For the present, I feel helpless. All that I can do is watch and wait. But I cannot help but wonder. . . .

Who *is* he? And what are his intentions?

CHAPTER THREE

In the life station aboard the *Battlestar Galactica*, Doctor Salik felt besieged by Starbuck and Apollo. The most exasperating thing for him was that he had no answers to give them. He was as puzzled by the situation as were they.

"Look," Apollo said, "we have all kinds of portable scanners. Surely you can get close enough to him to get a simple respiratory probe?"

"You could try that as well as I," said Salik, wearily. "It's a simple matter to get a reading."

"Yes," said Starbuck, "but—"

"But it didn't work," said Salik, cutting him off. He was growing tired of being badgered for things that didn't work, that weren't his fault. "I sent two of my best technicians to get close to him. They returned to me with broken scanners. I even sent Cassiopea."

"When all of our latest technology fails," Cassiopea said,

trying to lighten the tone in an effort to take some of the heat off Salik, "we resort to blatant feminine wiles."

"What happened?" said Starbuck.

"I think he's the most charming man I've ever met," she said.

"Oh, that's just wonderful!"

"That's on the outside," she said. "But I can't tell you a thing about what's going on behind that beautiful smile."

"Maybe you didn't get close enough to get a good scan on him," Apollo offered.

"Maybe we should discuss this without Starbuck around," Cassiopea said.

"Hey," said Starbuck, "it was all in the line of duty. Wasn't it?"

She shrugged. "I'd be lying if I told you that I wasn't impressed by him. There's something unbelievably compelling about Count Iblis. I was absolutely charmed. But I also came back with an empty tape."

She handed Starbuck a thin strip of silver mylar that she pulled out of the scanner. Starbuck held it up and squinted at it.

"What are you talking about, empty?" he said. "This heart rate is dancing around like a Cylon scanner!"

Cassiopea looked slightly sheepish.

"That's my pulse rate," she said. "This is his." She used a thin silver stylus to indicate the appropriate track.

"A straight line!" said Starbuck. "You really got to him!"

Salik shook his head and sighed in exasperation. He took the tape away from Starbuck, as if taking something away from a child because it was too young to play with it.

"It's not Cassiopea," he said. "It's the equipment. Either it's defective or . . . or he operates on some other wave length." He spread his hands out to his sides, then let them drop back down limply. "I don't know," he said. "I've never seen anything like it."

"There is another possibility," said Apollo thoughtfully. "That Count Iblis has some way of jamming our instruments. Doctor... is there any chance that this man... however handsome and charming," he added with an arch glance at Cassiopea, "is there any chance that he could be an android?"

"You mean some sort of machine, designed to look in every way like a man and programmed for certain response mechanisms?" said Salik.

"Exactly."

"Well, our own bio-robotics institutes were well advanced in that science, but I'm not the one to talk to. Doctor Wilker would be your best expert on that subject."

"I think a trip to the drone lab is in order," said Apollo.

"I'm with you," Starbuck said. "Let's go."

The shuttle had taken them to the Agro Ship, an old supply tanker so decrepit that even its name was unknown. When it had been commandeered during the mad flight from Caprica, the refugees were in no situation to pick and choose. No one had been able to read either its name or numerical designation, so worn was its hull. Its logbook could not be found and the spacers who refitted it en route as best they could from whatever parts were available and from whatever they could cobble up were, as many of their breed, superstitious about renaming a ship. It came to be known simply as the Agro Ship, which described its primary function, that of supplying the fleet with food for its journey.

Its massive cargo holds had been converted into crude

but functional greenhouse domes that were miles across. Besides serving as an agricultural plant for the fleet's galleys, the ship also served to provide a much needed link for the refugees with the verdant worlds they had left behind.

Sheba and Count Iblis strolled through a domed forest. The trees grew thick and tall, lovingly cared for by the laborers quartered in the lower decks of the Agro Ship. It was almost possible to believe that they were not on a ship, but walking through a leafy forest back on Caprica. It was the last bit of home that they had been able to take with them when they left their ravaged worlds behind.

"Isn't it lovely here?" said Sheba.

"A veritable garden," Count Iblis said.

"We brought a few of everything we could in the time that we had," said Sheba. "We had no idea what we could expect to find on Earth."

Iblis moved up to a tree and leaned against it, staring up at the dome, through which the stars were visible.

"What *can* we expect to find on Earth?" said Sheba, looking at him eagerly.

He smiled. "What do you wish to find?"

"A civilization strong enough to fight back against the Cylons," she said.

"Ah, that's not the quest which truly burns closest to your heart," said Count Iblis.

"Of course it is," she said, protesting. "It's what we all want. How would you know?"

"I *know* you," Iblis said softly. "I can *feel* you. And I am at this moment closer to your soul than any man has ever been." His eyes glittered as he gazed at her. Something deep within them seemed to burn. "Apollo is in your thoughts," he said, "but there is something . . . someone else even more important."

He reached out and took Sheba's hands, pulling her gently closer to him. She looked confused.

"You're unlike anyone I've ever met," she said.

"Think, Sheba," said Count Iblis. "Think with your soul and I will tell you your heart's desire. Ah, yes. Yes, of course. I should have known sooner. I will bring you together."

"With whom?"

"Why, your father, of course. The legendary Commander Cain. The Juggernaut who roams the stars. You will see him again."

"How could you possibly know what I'm feeling?" Sheba said, her voice little more than a whisper.

His eyes blazed at her.

"All people are capable of feeling one another's thoughts," he said. "It merely takes a little time and experience. Place your trust in me and I promise you, all things will become possible."

Sheba found that it was becoming difficult to breathe. Her lips felt dry. She moistened them with her tongue. Count Iblis pulled her closer. She swallowed hard and raised her face to his. He leaned down and kissed her lingeringly on the lips. She felt his lips part and, it seemed to her, almost involuntarily, her tongue entered his mouth. It felt like she was burning. She felt his arms go around her, pressing her body up against his. She went limp.

An old farmer who worked the Agro Ship entered the small clearing where they stood. They didn't notice him. He watched them for a moment, smiled, thought briefly about his youth, then disappeared once again into the trees, not wishing to intrude upon the couple.

A bright light suddenly illuminated Count Iblis and Sheba. She felt its warmth, even through the fire that she burned with.

They looked up.

A swarm of white hot lights raced across the blackness, outshining the stars.

"What is it?" Sheba whispered, staring up through the dome at the swirling lights that moved with astonishing speed. "What are they?"

"Don't be frightened," said Count Iblis. She felt his arms tighten around her. "They cannot hurt you as long as you're with me."

"Those lights," she whispered, hypnotized by their white hot glow, "they're truly beautiful. . . ."

"Don't be beguiled," said Count Iblis, a hard edge to his voice. "They taunt you with a glow that conceals everlasting darkness. Look away, Sheba."

She buried her head against his chest.

"How horrid. . . ."

"Yes, but you are safe with me," said Iblis. He was smiling. "They cannot touch you, so long as I am inside you."

On the bridge of the *Galactica,* there was a flurry of activity as the lights appeared. They raced past the ship, around it, swirling like a tornado of supernovas. Adama raced onto the bridge, having seen them through the observation port in his quarters.

"What *is* it?"

Tigh was staring at his scanners. He shook his head.

"We don't know, sir," he said. "There's not a thing on

any of our scanners, nothing at all. Not a blessed thing!"

"That's not exactly accurate, Colonel," said Athena. "They're here. They're just not here long enough for us to get a reading on them."

"They must be traveling at speeds beyond... beyond..." Tigh was at a loss for words.

"Yes, Colonel," said Adama, staring out the massive observation port at the white objects flashing across space and curling back around the *Galactica*, "beyond our comprehension."

"Commander," Rigel said, looking up from the scanners, "we're getting distress calls from every ship in the fleet. People are panicking."

"Put me on uni-com," said Adama.

"Uni-com activated."

"Attention, attention, this is Commander Adama to all ships in the fleet. Please maintain communication silence. I repeat, please maintain communication silence. There is no cause for alarm. The... ships... or manifestations we are encountering do not appear to be in any way hostile. Only by keeping the communication circuits free of random signals can we hope to utilize the full potential of our scanners. Blue Squadron, scramble precautionary intercept."

Starbuck and Apollo were in the drone lab, speaking with Doctor Wilker when the alert came on.

"Yes, it is possible to construct a lifelike android that would be most difficult to tell from a real human," Wilker was saying, "but there are ways of telling—"

The claxon began to sound.

"Not now, Doc," said Apollo. He started running for the door. "We'll be right back," he called over his shoulder.

"We hope," Starbuck added.

As they ran down the corridor toward the launch tubes, other pilots in Blue Squadron joined them.

"What is it?" Starbuck asked Boomer as they ran down the corridor together.

"Nothing like anything you've ever seen before," said Boomer.

Four of the Vipers in Blue Squadron had already launched by the time Starbuck, Boomer and Apollo arrived in the launch bay. They raced for their ships.

Greenbean and Bris were in wing formation as they piloted their Viper fighters toward the lambent intruders.

"Bris, do you see what I see?" said Greenbean.

"I'm afraid I do," came the reply over the helmet com-circuit.

"I don't know what the hell those things are," said Greenbean, "but I aim to find out. This is one time I'm going to beat Apollo to the point. Full power and let's go after them!"

They hit their engines, giving the ships everything they had as they took off in pursuit of the white hot lights that seemed to hover ahead of them. Suddenly their targets streaked away so quickly that they seemed to vanish.

"What the. . . . Where'd they *go?"* said Bris. "They simply vanished!"

"No," said Greenbean, awed by what he had seen. "They just left us standing virtually still compared to their speed. I've never seen anything like it!"

"So what do we do? Pursue or turn back?"

"Pursue *what?"* said Greenbean. "There's nothing on my scanner. I—"

At that moment, Greenbean's cockpit was bathed in an eerie white light. He turned to look behind him, since there was nothing on his scanner to explain the phenomenon. Just behind and above the four Viper fighters, an immense ship appeared seemingly out of nowhere. Greenbean cringed involuntarily. It felt as if a planet were falling down upon them, so massive was the alien ship. Before any of the pilots could react, they felt a sudden, piercing pain as if their bodies were all simultaneously grabbed by some giant fist and squeezed. The pressure was unbearable. Greenbean heard Bris start screaming just before he blacked out.

"Flight leader to bridge," Apollo said into his helmet mike, "flight leader to bridge, launched and ready to pursue. Give us coordinates. There doesn't seem to be anything out here."

On the bridge, Tigh frowned and turned to Adama.

"Commander?"

"I heard him," said Adama. "Tell wing control to give Captain Apollo the present coordinates of Greenbean's flight. They were in full pursuit."

"I'm sorry, Father," said Athena, licking her lips and shaking her head. She kept attempting to track the other pilots. "We don't *have* the present coordinates of Greenbean's flight."

"*What?* That's impossible! They just launched microns ago. How far out can they be? Even on full power, they just can't have . . ."

"Not very far," Athena said. "But they've disappeared off our scanners, I have no trace of them. It's as if they've simply been . . . plucked out of space."

"Just like Bojay's patrol," said Tigh.

Adama turned and walked away, feeling fury, frustration and resentment. How could he hope to fight something he couldn't even begin to understand?

"Sir?" said Tigh. "What do we tell our pilots?"

"Tell them to return to the *Galactica* at once," Adama said. "And cancel the red alert."

Tigh's voice came over the comcircuits in the Viper pilots' helmets.

"Blue Squadron recall, Blue Squadron recall. Return to the *Galactica*."

"What's he talking about?" said Starbuck, mystified. "We just got here."

"I don't know," Apollo said.

"And where're the others? Greenbean, Bris. . . . They launched just ahead of us. I don't see any sign of them on my scanner."

"I don't know that, either," said Apollo. "Boomer, exactly what was it you saw?"

"I was in the Officer's Club," said Boomer, "when everyone started shouting, hollering something about ships or machines or lights of some kind. I ran to the observation port and I saw them. It was incredible. Whatever they were, they were screaming by like meteorites. . . ."

"Maybe they were just meteorites," said Starbuck.

"Starbuck, their speed was *dazzling*," Boomer said. "And they were flying and turning in formation."

"Starbuck?" Apollo suddenly recalled where he had seen something like what Boomer had described.

"Just like what we saw down on that planet," Starbuck said.

"You saw them before?" said Boomer.

"Let's get back in," Apollo said. "We'd better get together with the commander."

They wasted no time in getting back to the *Galactica* and

meeting Adama in his quarters, where they told him about what they had seen down on the surface of the planet where they had found Count Iblis.

Adama was angry. "Why didn't you say something about those lights before?" He slammed his fist down onto the surface of his desk. "Why didn't you report them?"

"We thought perhaps we were caught in some sort of meteorite storm," Apollo said. "And frankly, Count Iblis pretty much had our full attention."

"Apollo," Starbuck said, thinking back to what had happened when they saw the lights, "didn't he say something about those lights being after him?"

Apollo nodded. "That's right. He did."

"And you didn't think that was important?" said Adama.

"Father...I thought he was as mad as a burned out drone. Nothing he said seemed to make any sense at the time. I thought he was in shock."

"What if he wasn't in shock?" said Adama. "What if he's telling the truth, that they're... beings that are pursuing him?"

Apollo shrugged helplessly. "I just don't know, Father. We've lost eight ships without a trace. I don't think we have a prayer of fighting these beings, whatever they are."

"I'll tell you one thing," said Starbuck. "I think it's past time to take off the diplomatic gloves. If this Count Iblis or whoever the hell he is is allowing us to send in fighters to be killed without a chance, then I for one don't think too much of him, not to put too fine a point on it. We have a right to know just what in hell is going on. He owes us some kind of explanation."

"Starbuck, you're dead right," said Adama. "We're fighting something we know nothing about. And that's about to change. Apollo, I want Count Iblis brought here at once."

Sheba and Count Iblis entered the deserted stadium aboard the *Rising Star*.

"And this is where your people play their games," said Iblis, looking around at the three-sided court.

"Triad," said Sheba. "It's more than just a game. It's a very important part of the mental well-being of our people. It gives them distraction, something to root for. A chance to win and be a part of something. A time to be away from the war and being caged up inside small metal ships."

"You needn't convince me," said Count Iblis. "I am a great believer in distraction." He turned to her and smiled. "Even pleasure," he added.

"What sort of games do they have where you come from?" Sheba said.

"Games that would amaze you. Games of life. Even games of death."

"How horrible . . ."

"Far from it," said Count Iblis. "Death is not an end. Only a beginning."

"You have a very dark side to you," said Sheba. "In some ways, you remind me of my father, of his love of war and conflict."

"A very perceptive observation."

"And what about the answer? Is the war of your choosing?" she said.

"I think Commander Adama would like to share in this discussion," said Apollo. Iblis looked up sharply to see Starbuck and Apollo standing at one end of the arena, watching them. "If you'll follow us. . . ." said Apollo.

"The conversation was between Sheba and myself," Iblis said, tensely.

"Count Iblis," said Apollo in a level tone, "you will either accompany me as a guest or as my prisoner. The choice is yours."

Something glittered in Count Iblis' eyes as he stared at Apollo.

"Apollo!" said Sheba, astonished at his actions. "I think you're being unforgivably rude! Of course the count will see Adama if that's his wish. Won't you?"

Iblis smiled at her. The chilling look he had given Apollo had disappeared as quickly as it had flickered across his features.

"Whatever you ask, my princess," he said.

He moved toward the door, past Apollo, without giving him a second glance. Sheba started to follow him, but Apollo reached out and took her by the arm, holding her back.

"Sheba, are you all right?"

"What are you talking about?"

"You," he said. "You don't seem yourself."

"How would *you* know?" she said angrily. "You never really knew me. This is the only man who truly *knows* me."

She pulled away from Apollo and went out past Count Iblis, who stood waiting in the doorway of the arena.

"Heed what I say to you, Apollo," Count Iblis said in an ominous tone. "Do not ever make the mistake of threatening me again. Or you will forfeit your life in the wink of an eye."

Starbuck's hand edged for his weapon. Apollo saw it and placed his hand gently on Starbuck's, restraining him. Count Iblis turned and angrily walked off down the corridor.

"Forget it, Starbuck," Apollo said. "There will be a better time. And I think our guest just revealed a hint of his true color."

Adama was waiting for them in one of the conference rooms aboard the *Galactica*. He was seated at one end of a long council table. Athena sat beside him, ready to record the meeting.

"Have a seat, Count Iblis," Adama said.

"Thank you." Iblis took a place at the far end of the table, opposite Adama.

"I have lost eight good people today," Adama said. "What do you know about it?"

"I told you that I could give you protection," Iblis said.

"How?"

"Follow me," Iblis said. "I will lead you all to safety."

"Who are you?"

"I am of another world. A level of being developed far in advance of you."

"How can you prove that?" said Adama, growing impatient with answers that were not answers.

"Prepare three tests for me," said Count Iblis. "And just as I can will that crystal in the center of this table to move . . ."

The ornamental crystal formation standing in the center of the table began to rise slowly as Iblis spoke.

". . . so can I deliver your people."

The crystal rose to a level with Adama's eyes, then gently settled to rest once again on the surface of the conference table. Adama looked at the crystal uneasily. It was quite heavy.

"I will ask you once again," he said, "who are you? And where do you come from?"

"Man has reached many levels in his evolutionary development," said Count Iblis, "some far greater than others. As you are, I once was. As I am, you may become."

"Who are you?" said Adama, once again, struggling to keep his temper in check. "Where do you come from?"

"I come from that place where man's ability to think, to comprehend, to will, is in its highest degree of accomplishment. We have learned to use the tools and opportunities of the mind to accomplish what you would deem miracles."

"That does not answer my question," said Adama.

Iblis smiled. "Adama, I converse with you out of courtesy. I know your questions before you ask them. I know your doubts, your suspicions, your grievances. This young man on my right, your son, thinks quickly of the pilots you lost. The deed was not mine. They were beyond my dominion. But that can change. If you will agree to follow me."

"To Earth?" said Adama.

"If that is your wish."

"But it is of no importance to you where we go?"

"If you see Earth as your destiny, then let us begin our voyage at once," said Iblis.

"Can you get our pilots back?" said Starbuck.

"That might present a problem."

"Even if we include it in the three tests you will grant us in exchange for your leadership?" Adama said.

"The wishes must extend from this point in time forward," said Count Iblis. "I cannot change that which already is."

Adama nodded. "You will have our decision," he said, rising from his chair.

"Soon, I trust," said Count Iblis. "The powers that you encountered this day will return again and again . . . until you are under my protection."

Adama looked down at Count Iblis, uncertain as to how to interpret his last remark. The interview had not produced the desired results. Quite the opposite, in fact. What worried him was that Count Iblis seemed to be playing with them. He seemed unconcerned. Adama wondered just how much power the man really had. He turned angrily and left the conference room. The others followed.

Count Iblis was left alone. He rose and slowly crossed the room to stand by the observation port. He looked out at the fleet and smiled.

FROM THE ADAMA JOURNALS:

Questions, questions and more questions. Never any answers. But at least there is one less question in my mind. Count Iblis is not from the planet Earth. He did not say as much, but I have no doubt in my mind.

He must know that all that it would take for him to achieve everything he seems to want would be to allow word to spread that he had come from Earth, to meet us and to bring us home. That one act would be like a piece of food to a starving man to all the people in the fleet. It would tell them everything they needed to know. It would convince even the cynical among them that Earth exists, that it is not just a fragment from some long forgotten legend that we are all pursuing. It would tell them that Earth exists, that there was a way to get there and that they were ready and waiting for us, to help us in our battle against the Cylon Empire. It would accomplish all of that and yet, Count Iblis isn't doing it. He could, of course, lie. Perhaps he is lying, but the one lie he isn't telling is the one that would give him complete control of the *Galactica*, command over the fleet. *Why?*

Why this charade of the three tests? Why play the role of some auditioning genie? It does not make sense. I am prepared to badger him with questions until hell freezes over, to force the answers out of him, but no. Something tells me that course could be dangerous.

He has powers we don't even suspect. That much is obvious. He told us so by moving that heavy crystal with his mind. It was not an elaborate demonstration, but it was an effective one. It could be that telekinesis is the limit of his powers, that he cannot do much more than what he has already shown us. It could be all a colossal bluff.

Why the three tests, if it is a bluff? The demonstration of the crystal was to tease us. To show us that there were things he was capable of doing that we could not do. The three tests, no doubt, will be further demonstrations. But, again, *why?*

If he can, indeed, do all the things he promised, if he is our superior in both powers and intelligence, why prove anything to us?

Why not simply take whatever it is he wants?

To all outward appearances, Count Iblis, if that is his name, is but one man. Yet I am afraid.

CHAPTER FOUR

A Cylon base ship was the Empire's equivalent of a Colonial battlestar, and a battlestar was what this base ship pursued. The pursuit was a relentless one, for it was unthinkable that the chase should be abandoned, unthinkable that even one human should be allowed to survive. The Imperious Leader of the Cylon Empire had decreed that the humans were to be exterminated. The command was for total annihilation and that meant to the last man, woman and child. The reasoning was simple. If the humans were able to reach some sort of haven, a world where they could start anew, they would begin to reproduce. They would flourish and their numbers would grow greater until they once again became a threat to the perfect order of the universe.

The Imperious Leader had determined that the task force would chase the human fleet until the end of time, if necessary, but the human parasites would be found and neu-

tralized. He would not go down in the history of the Empire
as the leader who had *almost* wiped out the human menace.
He would finish the job.

It pleased the Imperious Leader that the job of wiping
out the humans was being facilitated by one of their own
race. It was through the treachery of the human named
Baltar that the holocaust that had destroyed the twelve human worlds had been so effortlessly accomplished. Posing
as an emissary of peace, a go-between, the human turncoat
had lulled the Council of the Twelve into a false sense of
security so that when the attack came, the humans were
completely unprepared. That should have been the end of
it, yet a paltry group of survivors had escaped to flee across
space. It was a miracle that there should have been any
survivors at all. It was yet another example of the stubborn
nature of the human parasite, all the more reason why the
survivors had to be hunted down. It should have happened
a long time ago, but for the human commander, a man
named Adama.

Of all the humans left alive, Adama was the most dangerous. The Imperious Leader had underestimated him before. He would not do so again. The supreme Cylon knew
that just because the humans were inferior, that did not
mean that they were not complex. More than any other
Cylon in the history of the Empire, the Imperious Leader
understood the workings of the human mind, but still it was
not enough. A Cylon could not think like a human. And
to hunt down an enemy, it was necessary to know how that
enemy thought.

In an unprecedented move, the Imperious Leader had
turned over the command of a Cylon base ship to a human,
the human named Baltar. If anyone had reason to see Adama

dead, then Baltar was that man. Baltar hated the commander of the *Battlestar Galactica* with every fiber of his being. Two things would drive him to see the task through to its conclusion—his hatred of Adama and his fierce desire to prove himself useful to the Cylon Empire. The Imperious Leader knew that Baltar would persevere until the job was done. And then he would be disposed of. Baltar did not know that, but that did not matter. The mere fact that the human race could produce creatures capable of turning against their own kind was argument enough for their extermination. The Imperious Leader had vowed that the humans would be wiped out to the last man. That last man would be Baltar.

The Cylon base ship that hunted the *Galactica* was searching for signs of the human fleet, its scanners questing for traces of fuel residue that would tell Baltar which way the refugees had fled. They had slipped away from him before and he had found them; he would do so again. He was confident that they would find Adama and his pathetic fleet of junk ships. He was resting in his quarters, so he did not see the strange swarm of white lights that hurtled across space toward his base ship. His first warning that something was amiss came when the alarms blared throughout the ship. He instantly leapt to his feet and raced toward the command room, past Cylon Centurians running to their posts. Lucifer was waiting for him when Baltar arrived at the command center, out of breath.

"What is it? What's happening?" said Baltar, gasping for breath.

The I.L. series computer swiveled around to face him.

"We appear to have encountered something unexplainable," Lucifer said.

"What?"

"See for yourself. . . ."

Baltar moved up to stare at the scanners.

"But I don't see anything on these scanners," he said.

"That, I am afraid, is precisely the point," said Lucifer. "Our interceptors are reporting a large number of flying objects moving at incalculable speeds. They are all around us, and yet they are not registering on our monitors."

"Adama," Baltar said. "He has scientists aboard the *Galactica*. Perhaps they've made a technological breakthrough of some kind."

"Let us hope so," said Lucifer.

Baltar stared at the computer. "You would hope that the humans have made so advanced a breakthrough?" he said in astonishment.

"The alternative," said Lucifer, "is that we have encountered a new and more powerful force in the universe than our own."

Baltar allowed the implications of the statement to sink in. He found them frightening.

The freighter was never meant to carry human cargo. Cubicles were piled upon cubicles, creating cliff dwellings of metal one after another in row upon row upon row. It was a ghetto city built inside a ship, a city that was physical proof of the hardship of the journey. People were packed in like sardines, each doing their best to try to make a life for themselves in cobbled-together quarters. It was to these people that Count Iblis came.

He walked with Sheba through the "streets" of the city, passing children playing stick ram, an old woman weaving cloth, groups of men whose voices dropped to whispers at the sight of the female warrior and her white-clad companion.

As they passed, an old woman peered out from behind a cloth partition that gave some semblance of privacy to her pathetic cubicle.

"The people in these large freighters have fashioned dwellings for themselves as best they could," Sheba was saying, "but there is a constant shortage of materials and first priority must, unfortunately, go not to the living quarters but to the maintenance of ships and life support systems."

"It's appalling," said Count Iblis.

"Who asked you?" the old woman shouted at him.

"Please," said Sheba, looking at the woman kindly, "don't be rude. This man is our friend."

"Oh, is that so?" the old woman countered, her voice heavy with resentment. "And where is the count staying? What kind of food does *he* find on his table?"

"How did you know who—" Sheba began, but she was cut off by one of the men who had detached himself from the group they passed.

"Everyone has heard of the man who has come to us and talked of miracles," the man said in a challenging tone. "Tell us, Count, what do you do besides take up space and use up rations?"

"Yes, show us a miracle!" the old woman shouted. "Take my meager rations and multiply them!"

Count Iblis raised his eyebrows. "Is that all you would have me do?"

"When you have but a single talon plant to last a secton," the old woman said bitterly, "two such plants would be miracle enough!"

"Then you shall have two," said Count Iblis. "You shall have two multiplied by all the ships in the fleet if that be one of Adama's wishes."

"Just the sort of answer to our prayers we might expect," said the old woman scornfully. "We ask for food, we ask for a sign to lead us to Earth, we ask for safety from the Cylons and look what we are given. A madman."

A crowd had gathered around them, which was growing by the moment.

"Do not despair, old woman," said Count Iblis. "Stand tall. Your hunger will be appeased. Your safety and your destiny are assured. I give you my word."

"Your word! You are as trapped as we are!"

"I did not come here by chance," said Count Iblis. "Follow me and I will lead you to—"

"Adama is our leader."

Count Iblis turned to see Starbuck and Apollo standing among the crowd.

"Then why has he no compassion for these people?" Count Iblis said in a voice loud enough for all to hear. "They are living like animals."

"My father doesn't promise what no man can deliver," said Apollo.

"Your father has but to ask me and these people will have all the food and comforts they desire," said Count Iblis.

"Then forget Adama," shouted the old woman. "We'll follow you. If you can fill our cauldrons with food, if you can give us more heat, and if you can deliver us to Earth or anyplace else where we can live in peace."

"And if I do these things," Count Iblis said, "will you follow me?"

"We'll all follow you," a man shouted, "madman or not!"

Iblis turned to Apollo and smiled.

"There, Apollo," he said. "There you have your answer."

"Count Iblis," said Sheba, "how will you do as you say?"

He remained silent for a long moment.

"Go to the Agro Ship," he said finally. "See for yourself."

A murmur ran through the crowd. Starbuck and Apollo glanced at each other uneasily, then headed back to their shuttle.

The old farmer moved through the area of strange new growths and gazed about him with wonder. Exotic fruits hung from each tree in rich abundance.

"I can't explain it," the old farmer said with a tremor in his voice. "The trees have just begun to bloom and multiply overnight."

Apollo and Starbuck watched as Doctor Wilker moved up to one of the fruiting trees with a sensor device.

"Apollo, there has to be some rational explanation," Starbuck said, staring at the strange new growths.

"I want to bring samples of all these fruits and plants back with me to the *Galactica*," said Doctor Wilker.

"There has to be some logical explanation for this," Apollo said.

"Well, I can't give you one," said Wilker. "Something extraordinary has happened here."

"I'll tell you what it is," the old farmer said reverently. "It's a miracle, that's what it is. A miracle."

The two pilots walked down the corridor that led to the private quarters of Commander Adama. Apollo was deeply disturbed.

"Look at it this way," said Starbuck, "something wonderful is happening. We have more food, a guide to help us find our way across the stars. Why are we trying to make something sinister out of it?"

Apollo stopped and stared at Starbuck, as if not certain of what he heard.

"Because something inside of me is saying, 'don't trust him.' There's something wrong, Starbuck. I can *feel* it."

"I don't suppose it would have anything to do with the liking Sheba has taken to the good count, would it?" said Starbuck.

"Thanks, friend," said Apollo softly.

"Hey, I'm sorry," Starbuck said. "I know you better than that. But sometimes we feel things we don't even realize. I mean, we are all human."

"Not necessarily," Apollo said.

They reached Adama's quarters and, a moment later, were admitted.

"Father," said Apollo, "you've got to do something. Count Iblis has everyone convinced that he has supernatural powers."

Adama looked up from his desk. He looked very weary.

"What if he has?" Adama said.

"You don't mean that."

Adama got up slowly and moved to the star window. He stood silent for a moment, gazing out.

"Apollo," he said, "we're not alone in the universe. Who knows what manner of life exists out there? Can you assure me that the very Lords of Kobol who founded our civilization did not themselves come from some race which continued to evolve and advance at a far greater speed than our own?"

"Then why wouldn't they make themselves known to us?" said Starbuck.

Adama glanced at him. "Maybe they have."

"Count Iblis?" said Apollo.

"He could be our first contact with our fathers," said Adama.

"A parent race that's far in advance of us?" said Starbuck. "That's a frightening thought."

"Why?" said Adama.

"Because we'd be powerless to control our own destiny from this point forward if that's true," Starbuck said.

"I'm not so sure," Adama said. "If you've noticed, Count Iblis has asked us to follow him. He has not commanded it."

"Maybe that's next," said Apollo.

"Maybe that's not possible."

Apollo frowned. "Meaning, we have to submit to him of our own free will?"

"That's what makes me think he comes from the same roots as our own race," said Adama. "Freedom of choice, to choose between right and wrong has always been the cornerstone of our faith, of our civilization."

"You make it sound as if Count Iblis is some sort of god, Father."

Adama nodded, considering his son's words. "Perhaps, in a way, he is. I'm certain that we would appear like gods to a race far more primitive than ourselves. He may be no more than a man, but a man from another time, with great powers and great strengths. But also governed by rules."

"What are you going to do?" Apollo said. "The people are ready to follow him, whatever he is."

"He asked me to prepare three tests of his powers," said Adama. "I'm going to do just that."

• • •

Count Iblis entered the reception hall. Seated before him, on a level slightly above that of the rest of the chamber, were twelve men.

"Count Iblis," said Adama, rising to his feet, "may I present our Council of Twelve? If we are to turn our destiny over to you, it is they who must make the final decision."

Count Iblis nodded.

"You have agreed on three tests of my strength," he said, addressing them all. "The first is to deliver your enemy, the second is to accurately plot your course to Earth. The third . . . the third you cannot agree on. Some of you wish to know who I am and where I come from. Others are satisfied to accept me on the strength of my works and follow blindly provided I guarantee your safety."

The members of the council were shocked and astonished.

"There is no way he could have known," said Montrose to the others. "Only now did we voice our choices and put them to a vote!"

Count Iblis smiled. "You, Sire Edbryn," he said, looking directly at the junior member of the council. "You seem most skeptical of all, with the possible exception of Commander Adama and his son, who escorted me here. Therefore, I am willing to grant your first wish before you have decided on the third. I will deliver your enemy unto you. This very night."

He walked over to the large star window and gazed out into space intently. The chamber was completely silent.

• • •

Baltar sat brooding in the throne room aboard the Cylon base ship. He looked up as Lucifer entered, gliding silently across the floor.

"Any further news of these machines?" said Baltar. "These creatures or manifestations or whatever in Kobol's name they are?"

"Our attack craft are unable to pursue them," Lucifer said. "Whatever they may be, they are too swift for us."

"Prepare my personal craft and crew," said Baltar.

"To what end?"

"Send out a long-range signal, unidirectional, to the *Galactica,* wherever she is. Notify her that I wish to rendezvous with her. They may send out Viper interceptors to make sure that I come alone under the universal signal of truce."

"You expect to be treated according to universal law after all you've done to them?" said Lucifer.

"It is my life that I risk," said Baltar. "Do as I ask."

"By your command," said Lucifer, gliding backwards out of the chamber.

Adama stood tensely behind the scanner station next to Colonel Tigh.

"Bring the fleet to full alert," he said to his executive officer.

"Yes, sir."

"What is it, Father?" said Apollo, entering with Starbuck. "What's going on?"

"We've just received a direct communique from Baltar," said Adama. "He's asked to come aboard the *Galactica* under the universal sign of truce."

"*Baltar!*" said Apollo. "Here! Aboard the ship!"

"It has to be a trick," said Starbuck. "A ruse to find us and attack. Let me take a squadron out and give him a real hot reception!"

"It doesn't appear to be a trick," Adama said. "He's coming alone and unescorted. He says he will follow any course directions we might give him, so that he can be intercepted."

"That's incredible," said Apollo. "You don't think this has anything to do with the promise made by Count Iblis?"

"I don't know what to think," Adama said.

"If you ask me," said Starbuck, "it's got everything to do with it. And it's nothing supernatural. This is some kind of plan to get inside our defenses and Baltar and Count Iblis are both working together."

"The irony of it is that I wish I believed it were that simple," said Adama. "In any case, we will take every precaution. Launch Blue Squadron to bring Baltar aboard."

It was an event unlike anything we'd experienced since the destruction of our civilization. Baltar's ship reached our sector and was immediately intercepted by Apollo's elite squadron, who escorted the treasonous instrument of our holocaust directly into our hands.

Word spread like sunbursts through every corner of the fleet. It was a jubilation unprecedented as Baltar was brought before the Council of the Twelve.

It was just as Count Iblis had promised. Our enemy had been delivered unto us.

It was well known throughout the fleet that Count Iblis said he would submit to three tests we were to impose upon him. Count Iblis had made certain that it was well known. And it was equally well known that the first such feat he promised to perform was to deliver our enemy to us. Was it coincidence? If so, it was an incredible one. And, if it *was* a coincidence, no one in the fleet seemed to believe it. The people were convinced that Baltar's surrender had been brought about through the powers of Count Iblis. I was not convinced.

But what if it were true?

CHAPTER FIVE

Baltar stood in the council chamber, before the assembled Council of the Twelve. Several of them he knew, as they had been the members of the original council whom he had betrayed. These men stared at him with a burning hatred in their eyes. He had come to them once before, speaking on behalf of the Cylon Empire, holding out the hope of peace. Instead, he had brought them death and devastation. The others of the council Baltar did not know, for they had been elected from among the survivors of the holocaust. These men had not seen Baltar before, at least not in the flesh, but each and every one of them knew full well who and what he was. Their hatred of him was no less than that of the few remaining members of the original Council of the Twelve. If looks could kill, then Baltar would have fried upon the spot.

Sire Montrose was one of those men who knew Baltar

from before. He rose from his seat, his face a pale mask of fury.

"Baltar," he said, struggling to keep his voice under control, "you have been found guilty of treason against the state and in violation of every code of moral and ethical conduct of mankind. It frightens me when I think of what I, personally, would like to do to you, but we are bound by laws. The worst punishment I can mete out to you is, in my opinion, nowhere near harsh enough, but I will be bound by the limit of our laws. You are sentenced to spend the remainder of your life in confinement aboard the prison barge."

"No!" said Baltar, the color draining from his face. "No, I say, you cannot do this! I came to you under a sign of truce!"

"As you came before the Council once before, under a sign of truce?" said Montrose. "A *Cylon* truce?"

"You need me," Baltar said. "We need each other. There is a power greater than yours, greater than all the Cylon Empire! It will destroy us if we do not unite!"

"May I address the Council?" said Count Iblis.

"With the Council's permission," said Montrose. He glanced around at his fellow members. They all nodded their assent.

Count Iblis rose to his feet and moved to stand in front of Baltar. He looked like some avenging angel in his flowing white robes.

"Baltar," he said softly, "there is nothing you or your Cylon friends can do to combat the powers of which you speak."

"What do you know of these powers?" Baltar said. "They defy description."

Count Iblis smiled. "I know these powers as well as I know you, Baltar."

The traitor frowned. "You do not know me. Who are you?"

"I am Count Iblis, and I lead these people from your clutches, just as I led you to surrender to their justice."

"I came here of my own free will," said Baltar.

"Just as I bring you to your knees and command you to accept their punishment," said Count Iblis, gazing directly at Baltar with eyes that seemed to blaze.

Something changed in Baltar's face. He began to shiver, his knees began to buckle. Count Iblis stood before him, smiling slightly. Baltar's face broke out into a sweat as he strained against a power he did not understand. Tears began to stream from his eyes as he sank down to his knees against his will and bowed his head in submission.

"Remove him," said Adama.

Two guards came up to Baltar and dragged him from the chamber. He did not understand what had happened to him. There was an expression of fear mixed with confusion on his face. He could not stop weeping.

"There were two more prerequisites to our bargain," said Count Iblis, turning to face the Council. "One . . . that I would lead you to Earth. The other . . . to be decided amongst you. What is your decision?"

Sire Edbryn spoke.

"Count Iblis, what has transpired here is, I am sure, an inspiration to all of us. I ask you to give us time to consider that which we will propose."

"I believe that I have already proven myself worthy of your trust," said Count Iblis. "How long will this consideration take?"

"Not long, Count Iblis. Not long."

"Very well. It shall be as you wish. I remind you that your people are expectant. Now, they rejoice in the fall of Baltar. But soon, they will expect the journey to Earth to begin. And they know that I can lead them there. When you have decided, you will find me among the people, in celebration. And anticipation."

His eyes briefly met Adama's before he turned and left the chamber.

"I believe that we should all join in the celebration," said Sire Montrose. "And I see no reason to delay electing Count Iblis to the presidency of our body. Are there any dissenting votes?"

"My dear brothers," said Adama, "if I may...."

They all gave him their attention.

"There are still unanswered questions," said Adama, spreading his arms out to his sides in a gesture of resignation, showing them that he could not understand their desire to act so quickly. "We have warriors who are still missing, probably dead, and a number of disquieting events to be studied. May I suggest an adjournment until tomorrow at this time?"

"I suppose one day more would not offend Count Iblis," said Sire Montrose. "But tomorrow, we convene under his leadership. Is that agreed?"

"Barring any disturbing factors to the contrary," said Adama, warily.

"Fair enough," said Sire Montrose. "The Council of the Twelve stands adjourned."

Adama was sitting alone in his quarters, thinking. He could not see any way to prevent the Council from giving the leadership of the fleet to Count Iblis and he knew that it was wrong. He felt it in his bones. He was certain that there was something about Count Iblis that none of them were seeing, but he simply did not know how to prevent it. How was it possible to fight against a man who seemed to have supernatural powers? If, indeed, he was a man.

Athena entered.

"Father? Come with me," she said. "I want you to attend the games."

"I'm sorry, Athena," said Adama morosely. "I can't think of the games at a time like this."

"Father, you sound just like Apollo," she said. "He's decided not to play tonight. It's almost started a revolution within the ships. He's going to be breaking up the most popular team."

"So that's why you want me there," Adama said, smiling. "To convince Apollo to play."

"Father, I don't think you understand how much these games have come to mean to everyone," Athena said. "At least you have command to occupy your thoughts. Some of these people have nothing but the games to look forward to."

"Yes," said Adama, "and I've heard that the wagering and rivalries are causing trouble within the fleet."

"Tonight is a special game. A championship. If Apollo doesn't play...."

Adama sighed. "Very well. I can't force him to compete. But I will speak to him."

"Thank you, Father."

Starbuck sat on a bench before his locker, wrapping his hands in polymesh tape as Boomer came in and sat beside him to change for the game.

"Without Apollo," Boomer said, "I believe I'm about to win my first championship."

"Thanks for the confidence, Boomer," Starbuck said, "but I can take you even with a substitute."

"You're taking this pretty well for a guy about to lose a championship over some petty jealousy," said Boomer.

"Apollo's not playing hasn't got anything to do with Count Iblis and Sheba," Starbuck said. "I don't feel any better about playing this game than Apollo. Eight of our best men have disappeared without a trace, we're about to turn over the command of the fleet to some stranger we know nothing about, simply because he's pulled some sort of hocus pocus that's pulled the wool over the eyes of everyone in the Council but Adama and here we are, wagering, laughing, shouting. . . . It doesn't seem right."

"But you're going through with it," said Boomer.

"Yeah, well, you and I get out of these metal boxes once in a while. It keeps us from going crazy. What about the rest of the people in the fleet? Some of them have nothing else in their lives except the little entertainment that these games provide."

He finished wrapping his hands, then slipped the gloves on.

"Besides," Starbuck added, "it helps me get rid of some of my hostilities. So look out."

The spectators were beginning to file into the stadium as Starbuck walked out onto the court. Doc Hansen, a young bearded med tech, waited for him nervously.

"What do you say, Doc?" said Starbuck. "Ready to play with the big boys?"

Hansen did not look happy. He shook his head sadly and

glanced up at the stands nervously.

"I don't know, Starbuck," he said. "Are you sure you wouldn't be better off playing with someone else?"

Starbuck frowned. "What's gotten into you?"

Hansen once again looked up at the rapidly filling stands. He saw that some people were staring back down at him, puzzled.

"Apollo's your teammate," Hansen said. "These folks are waiting to see you and *Apollo* play."

"Well, Apollo doesn't want to play," said Starbuck. "There's not much I can do about that. You'll just have to do the best you can, that's all."

"That isn't what I'm worrying about," said Hansen. "When these folks find out that *I'm* going to be your partner instead of Apollo, they're going to lynch me!"

"Hmmm," said Starbuck. "I hadn't thought of that."

"What should I do?" said Hansen, growing more upset by the moment.

"Try shaving off your beard and walkin' around like you've got a broomstick up your ass," said Starbuck. "Maybe that'll fool 'em."

Apollo was lying on his bunk in his quarters, staring up at the ceiling. The door to his cabin opened and his adopted son, Boxey, entered with his daggit droid, Muffy. Apollo sat up.

"Boxey! I've been looking all over for you. Where've you been?"

The boy continued to stare at Apollo without saying anything. After a moment, he turned and started to walk out again.

"Boxey, hold on. . . ."

The boy paid no attention. Apollo quickly jumped up and ran in front of the door, blocking his son's exit. Boxey wouldn't even look at him.

"Young man, I was talking to you," Apollo said. "Now since when do you just walk out without giving me a hug?"

Apollo started to pull the boy close to him, but Boxey strained against him, pulling away. Apollo frowned. He looked intently into the boy's eyes.

"Boxey . . . what is it? This isn't like you. We've always talked straight to each other, you and I. What's bothering you?"

No answer.

"Maybe you'll tell me, Muffy." Apollo reached his hand out to the droid in an attempt to lighten the moment. "What's the matter with Boxey?"

The daggit droid started backing up and growling at him.

"Hey, now what *is* this?" said Apollo, beginning to grow angry. "What's going on? Now, I mean it. I want an answer right this micron."

Boxey looked down at the floor.

"My friends all say that you're a coward," the boy said in a small voice.

"A coward? Boxey . . . you aren't serious. Why would they say a thing like that?"

"They say you're afraid to play in the games," said Boxey. "That you're afraid of losing."

"Afraid?" said Apollo. He reached out and took hold of the boy's arms. "Why would I be afraid? We've got the best team in the fleet. We can beat anybody."

"Count Iblis says that Boomer's team is going to win."

"Since when does Count Iblis know anything about triad?" said Apollo.

"They're saying that you're afraid that if you lose, it'll prove that Count Iblis is smarter than your father. That he should be our new leader. I don't want my father to be a coward," Boxey said.

"Look, son," said Apollo, "I know it's a little complicated for a young boy to understand, but my not playing in the games has nothing to do with my father. It has to do with wasting my time and laughing and carrying on like nothing is wrong while friends of mine may be out there dying someplace. Now can you understand that?"

Boxey lowered his head.

"I . . . I guess so."

"Good," said Apollo. "Now you go and tell your friends that I said it doesn't matter who wins the games. They're there to be enjoyed. And I'd be just as happy to see Boomer win for a change."

Boxey nodded and turned to go. At that moment his daggit droid began to growl. The boy glanced up to see Adama standing in the doorway. As he stepped into the light, the droid's visual sensors recognized him and the daggit, appropriately responding to programming, barked and wagged its tail.

"He didn't mean to growl at you, Commander," Boxey said, apologetically. "He just didn't recognize you at first. He's a good daggit, he really is."

Adama chuckled. "Of course he is." He kneeled down and the droid waddled over to him, nudging his chest and making artificial panting noises. "There, boy, ha-ha, there you go," said Adama, laughing and pummeling the droid. "You're a good daggit, aren't you, boy? A good old droid." He rose. Now you run along and do as your father said."

"Yes, sir," said Boxey. "Come on, Muffy."

The little droid scurried after the boy. Adama glanced up at Apollo and smiled.

"It isn't easy, is it, son?" he said.

"No," said Apollo, shaking his head. "How can I explain my feelings to a small child when I can't even explain them to myself?"

"I thought you did a good job," said Adama. "I'm not sure you're right, but you were honest. That's all anyone can ask."

"You, of all people, think that I should play?" Apollo said.

Adama sat down on the bunk beside his son.

"Is it going to serve any purpose to sit alone in your quarters and think about those missing warriors?" he said.

"Why don't we send out another patrol?" Apollo said.

"And lose them, too?"

"Then let me force Count Iblis to tell us what's happening," Apollo said. "I can't believe that those ships simply disappeared. If they'd exploded, we'd have found traces of debris, something. Our scanners should have picked up some sign of them. I think those white ships or whatever they are have something to do with it. And with Count Iblis. I *know* he knows where our warriors are!"

"Dealing with Count Iblis is my responsibility," Adama said. "Don't make it more difficult for me. Don't give me a fleet full of outraged enthusiasts because my son wouldn't show up to play in the championship. It would only further serve Count Iblis."

"That never occurred to me," Apollo said.

"He's already a very popular man," Adama said. "I think half the fleet is ready to follow him right now."

"Well, if my not playing in the games is going to shift

the balance his way," said Apollo, "then I guess I've got to play."

"You won't be doing our missing warriors a disservice," said Adama. "You may even be helping them."

Apollo stood up and nodded. Adama got up and embraced his son.

"Okay, I'll play," Apollo said, "but on one condition. You have to watch the games."

"Accepted," said Adama.

A very relieved Hansen fled back to the locker room when Apollo walked out onto the court to a standing ovation. As soon as the crowd had realized that Hansen would be taking Apollo's place, they had booed him and cans of baharri had rained down upon him. He had lost his temper and called them a bunch of combrids with nictitating membranes and it had only resulted in more garbage being thrown. When Apollo arrived, Hansen was only too glad to leave the court.

"Well, so much for my moment of glory," Boomer said, seeing Apollo walk out on the court.

Sheba and Count Iblis sat in the first tier just behind and above him. Count Iblis leaned down.

"Well, this is a bit of a surprise," he said. "I didn't expect that he would show up."

"Well, he has and there goes the game," said Boomer.

"Don't give up before you even begin, Boomer," Sheba said. "You're good."

"Apollo's better," Boomer said. "I'd give anything to beat him and Starbuck just once."

"I'd heard you felt that way," Count Iblis said. "Maybe I can help."

Boomer shook his head. "Nothing can beat skill."

"The commander's son is a bit too sure of himself," Count Iblis said. "That weakness can be exploited."

"I can see you've never played triad against Starbuck and Apollo."

Count Iblis smiled. "I'd like to," he said. "Through you. How badly do you want to win?"

Boomer stared at Count Iblis long and hard. The claxon sounded the ready call and the two teams moved to take their positions.

Adama entered the stadium and sat down in the first tier, opposite Count Iblis. The two men looked across at each other. There was determination in Adama's face. He stared at Count Iblis with an unwavering glare. Something in Count Iblis' eyes seemed to glitter.

A hush settled down over the spectators' gallery as the players on the triad court took their positions. Boomer and Apollo were in the forward positions, facing each other across the starting line. Starbuck was playing back. Apollo glanced at Boomer's teammate. Boomer had chosen to play with none other than the young junior council member, Edbryn. Of course, Boomer had to play with a substitute. His regular partner, Greenbean, was. . . .

Edbryn looked a little nervous. Still, the junior council member had never been one to put on any great show of emotions. He was steadfast and level-headed, liked by everyone in the fleet. More than once, his dry sense of humor had scored points on Starbuck and Apollo, who both seemed to him to be a bit on the flamboyant side. Nevertheless, what he undertook to do, he did to his utmost and, although he had never played in a championship triad game before, Apollo knew that he would go all out. Apollo saw him standing on the far side of the court, his legs slightly spread, his eyes alert, his long hair held by a lithium clasp at the nape of his neck. It would be an interesting match, Apollo thought, with Edbryn pitted against Starbuck. The two were completely opposite in every way. Edbryn would be a competitive player, Apollo thought, but his chief concern would be with Boomer. Boomer was good and Boomer wanted desperately to win. Apollo almost wanted to let him. He realized how much it would mean to Boomer, but he also knew that Boomer was a good enough player to realize if he were being given in to. No, Apollo would have to play all out. Besides, it was the only way he knew how to play.

The two forwards squared off against each other. It was completely silent in the stadium.

The claxon sounded the start of the game.

Almost at the same instant that the claxon sounded, Boomer lashed out with a swift and brutal side kick directly into Apollo's solar plexus. So quickly had Boomer moved, Apollo had been taken completely by surprise. It seemed to him that Boomer jumped the gun, but there was no time to speculate on that. Even through the polymesh protective vest he wore, Apollo felt the incredible force of the kick. Momentarily winded, he doubled over and, as he did so, Boomer came down on him with a savage overhead blow that landed on Apollo's nysteel helmet. The helmet protected Apollo from injury, but even so, it felt like a gong went off inside his head. For a moment, he saw stars and he fell to the floor. Boomer was by him in an instant, moving on the offensive. The only thing between him and the ball was Starbuck.

"*Kobol*, Boomer was a little rough there, wasn't he?" Athena said, wincing at the blow he had dealt to Apollo.

"There was no need for that second blow, he could have gotten by him after the first one."

"Well, Boomer *did* say he wanted to win," said Sheba. "I guess he decided to pull out all the stops."

Count Iblis sat perfectly still, leaning forward, staring down at the court with a wild intensity. If those who sat near him had not been so absorbed in the game, they might have been startled by the savagery of his expression. His eyes were blazing with an unholy light.

Starbuck had been shocked at the fury of Boomer's assault on his teammate and the speed with which it had been executed. Still, it was a rough game and Starbuck knew that Boomer wanted to win the championship more than anything. The spectators had erupted into wild shouting when Apollo went down. Boomer charged across the line. Apollo was still stunned. Starbuck steeled himself for the confrontation, knowing that with Apollo still out of the game, he was the only thing that stood between Boomer and Edbryn making the first score.

The moment that Boomer touched the ball, Starbuck *moved*. He hurtled across the court at Boomer.

Edbryn was also moving, getting into position to take a pass from Boomer and make a shot.

The circles began to flash upon the walls.

Boomer saw Starbuck coming at him hard. He cocked his right arm and hurled the nysteel ball with all his might, directly at Starbuck's unprotected face.

Starbuck sensed, rather than saw, what was coming. Yahrens of training and experience as a crack Viper pilot had given him lightning-quick reactions. As he ran, unable to slow his momentum, he *felt* the ball coming at him and ne planed out into a forward dive, passing only inches beneath the ball. Had he not flattened out into the dive, the nysteel ball would have struck him right in the face, rupturing flesh, shattering bone, very possibly even killing him if it hit just right.

The ball passed over him and slammed into the wall, rebounding crazily. Edbryn leaped for it, caught it in his polymesh gloves and spun around, flinging it at a lit five circle. The ball struck on target and the bell sounded, announcing the score. The crowd cheered, but there were a few dissenting voices expressing their disapproval of Boomer's highly unorthodox tactics.

Edbryn ran, jumped, and caught his own rebound.

Apollo was rising to his feet, shaking his head like a stunned bull, trying to clear his blurry vision.

Starbuck got up off the floor.

"Boomer!" he said. *"What the hell—"*

The ball was still in play.

Edbryn passed to Boomer.

Boomer caught the ball and turned, continuing the same motion, using the hand holding the ball to knock Starbuck off his feet again even as he spoke.

Starbuck felt the blow of nysteel against the side of his helmet and rolled with it, diffusing some of its impact. Boomer had gone crazy, he thought as he went down.

Boomer jumped up and shot the ball with both hands at an empty section of the wall. To the crowd, it appeared as though he was throwing the ball away, but just before it hit the wall, a ten circle flashed on and the ball struck home. The bell sounded and Boomer's team was leading by fifteen. The crowd went wild.

"How did he know the ten would flash on just then?"
said Athena. "He couldn't *possibly* have anticipated th
computer!"

Sheba shrugged. "Just lucky, I guess."

Count Iblis smiled slowly.

Adama frowned. The triad games had always been prett
rough, but this was getting out of hand. Boomer was com
pletely carried away and he was playing way beyond th
margin of safety. He wanted to stop the game, but to d
so would surely cause a riot. He sat back in his seat an
set his teeth. He watched his son, who had finally recovere
enough to get back into the game.

Apollo had taken the rebound. He was still a little woozy
What in the name of Kobol had gotten into Boomer? Thi
was getting serious, he thought. The first chance he go
he'd try to tell Boomer to relax, to loosen up. This wa
going too far. The crowd was becoming dangerously agi
tated.

Edbryn took position to cover Starbuck, trying to preven
a pass from Apollo. They jockeyed for position, Starbuc
trying to fake him out and get clear, Edbryn trying to sta
with him.

Boomer was bearing down on Apollo.

"Boomer," said Apollo, "will you for God's sake . . .
his voice trailed off.

There was a completely blank expression on Boomer'
face. He appeared to be in some sort of shock, moving lik
some somnambulistic juggernaut.

Boomer slammed into Apollo at top speed, smashin
them both into the wall. Apollo held onto the ball with a
his might. He almost dropped it, just the same, so hard di
Boomer hit him.

Wrenching to the side, Apollo jerked the ball away with both hands, then pivoted sharply, slamming the ball into Boomer's side.

Boomer went down.

And started getting up almost immediately.

The force with which Apollo hit him should have put him out of action for at least several microns, but he was getting up! It was as if the blow had no effect at all.

Apollo quickly passed to Starbuck.

"Boomer! Snap out of it! What's wrong with you?"

Edbryn intercepted the pass.

The crowd was making a noise louder than the whine of a Viper engine.

Starbuck was on Edbryn, not giving him a clear opportunity to try a scoring shot.

Boomer looked at Apollo. Stared right through him.

"Boomer?"

Edbryn snapped a pass into the wall. It hit, bounced, came spinning toward Boomer and Apollo.

Apollo jumped for it.

Boomer reached out, grabbed Apollo by the hips and yanked him down, smashing him viciously into the floor. He caught the ball.

The claxon sounded, ending the period. The game was half over and Boomer and Edbryn were leading, fifteen points to zero.

Starbuck ran over to Apollo, who had hit the floor on his knees. He was grimacing with pain. Starbuck reached out and helped him to his feet. The crowd was screaming.

"Has Boomer gone crazy?" Starbuck shouted at Apollo, so that his teammate could hear him over the din of the crowd.

"I don't know," Apollo shouted back, gasping with pain. "He's playing like a man possessed. He looks completely out of it."

"Out of it? What do you mean?"

"I don't know. I've never seen him like this. Something strange is happening. . . ."

"You're telling me?" Starbuck shouted back. "We're getting killed here."

Apollo managed a weak grin. "Funny you should put it that way. . . ."

On the other side of the court, Edbryn approached Boomer with an expression of concern on his face.

"Look, Boomer," he shouted, barely making himself heard, "aren't you overdoing it a bit?"

Boomer turned a blank expression to him. His eyes fluttered, then he shook his head. He looked puzzled, confused. The ready call sounded to begin the final period. Looking dazed, Boomer moved off to take the rear position for the second half. Frowning slightly, Edbryn walked to the center of the court to face off against Starbuck.

The claxon sounded to begin the play.

This time, Edbryn and Boomer were the defensive team. Starbuck had to get by Edbryn in order to put the ball into play. There was no time to waste, they were fifteen points behind.

Starbuck feinted to one side and when Edbryn moved to block him, Starbuck easily slipped by him. The crowd applauded his finesse. He ran across the court and picked up the ball, spinning around to pass it off the wall to Apollo. Edbryn was blocking him.

Starbuck threw the ball over Edbryn's head. It almost

sailed into the spectator stands. It hit the wall near its top rim, bounced off and shot across the court to Apollo.

Apollo saw that Boomer was positioned behind him, ready to slam into him the moment he tried for the ball. He flexed his legs, as if to jump, and the moment he felt Boomer's hands upon him, he swiveled around and flipped Boomer over his hip. The tactic, however, caused him to miss the ball. It flew into the wall behind him and rebounded again. Edbryn recovered it. He turned and shot.

The bell rang, score on a four circle. Nineteen to zero.

Starbuck got the rebound. The ball was still in play. There was bedlam in the stands. The crowd was witnessing an upset. Starbuck tried a shot and scored.

Nineteen to five.

Boomer had the ball. Apollo saw the same, blank unfocused stare on Boomer's face. He moved forward to block whatever Boomer tried, be it a shot or a pass. Boomer threw the ball at him.

Apollo jerked his head away just in the nick of time. He felt the breeze as the ball passed a fraction of an inch away from his cheekbone. The ball hit the wall behind him and bounced back hard, slamming into his back. He was knocked off his feet by the impact. As he looked up at Boomer, the adrenalin rush hit and everything seemed to shift into slow motion.

Adama saw the ball hit his son and he sat up straight, on the edge of his seat. What was Boomer thinking of? Had he gone insane or . . .

Apollo saw Boomer retrieve the ball. Everything seemed to be happening very slowly. Boomer looked like he was moving through some kind of thick, invisible soup. The roar of the crowd sounded very far away. He saw the ball float out of Boomer's hands, coming toward him. He had all the time in the world. Slowly, he raised his gloved hand and batted the ball away before it could strike him.

"Come *on*, Apollo," Athena urged from the stands, "get up! Get *up!*"

Apollo started rising to his feet.

Adama was leaning forward, on the edge of his seat. He looked across the court, at the stands on the other side.

"Iblis. . . ."

As if he had heard him, Count Iblis glanced up and their eyes met. Adama stared at him with a cold fury. Count Iblis smiled.

Everything shifted back into perspective for Apollo. The noise of the crowd suddenly grew tremendously in volume and the thick, invisible soup was gone.

Starbuck had recovered the ball, outmaneuvering Edbryn. He shot. The ball struck an eight circle and the bell rang, although the crowd was by this time so loud that no one heard its sound. The scoreboard registered the hit, nineteen to thirteen.

Apollo caught the rebound. Boomer stood in front of him, swaying slightly, his eyes fluttering. He looked disoriented. Apollo brushed by him and tried to pass to Starbuck. He was being effectively blocked by Edbryn.

Apollo tried a shot.

The three circle lit up.

Apollo threw.

The ball hit dead on target.

Nineteen to sixteen.

The claxon sounded, ending the game. Boomer's team had won. The crowd went berserk. Spectators jumped down onto the court to mob the winning team. Apollo glanced up at where Count Iblis had been sitting.

The seat was empty.

CHAPTER SIX

The lounge of the *Rising Star* was a scene of celebration. As was usual following a triad game, the recreation ship was crowded to capacity as everyone who did not have other pressing duties to attend to came to party. The bar was doing a brisk business, especially since the new yield in the Agro Ship enabled the crew of the *Rising Star* to augment its usual meager selection of wines and baharri. Boomer was enjoying the full fruits of his victory, basking in the attention paid him by the triad fans. In a corner, as if holding court over the dancing, drinking couples, Count Iblis was seated comfortably with Sheba curled up beside him. Two more woman reclined at his feet, completing the Dionysian scene.

It was not unusual for there to be merrymaking in the lounges of the *Rising Star*, especially following a triad championship. However, there was something about the atmosphere in the lounge that gave the revelry an altogether different sort of flavor on this occasion. The spirit of the partygoers was almost orgiastic. They were drinking more than usual, they were being louder than they usually were, there was a greater sense of abandon in the way they danced.

Count Iblis was pleased with the way things were turning out. He reached out and stroked Sheba's hair absently, but his hand hesitated when he saw Starbuck and Apollo standing in the entrance to the lounge. There was something feral about the expression on his face.

"Is it just me," said Starbuck to his friend, "or does everybody seem especially festive to mark the occasion of our loss?"

"I sure don't remember being this happy myself," said Apollo, surveying the scene. "Not even when we won."

"There is a new air of optimism, my two young friends," said Count Iblis, rising to greet the two pilots. "Why not join in it? You two look far too serious. The games will be but a distant memory before the night is through."

"Just how long is this party going to last?" said Apollo, with a touch of concern. "It looks like they're gearing up to go on for centons. Some of these people are in critical jobs."

Count Iblis smiled. "Trust me to worry about the fleet from now on, gentlemen. It is my commandment that everyone here live life to its fullest."

"No matter how long it lasts," said Starbuck.

Sheba shook her head in exasperation. "Apollo, Starbuck, you guys just don't seem to be getting the point," she said. "We're all saved." She spoke to them as if she were addressing two children who were slow to understand what was being explained to them. "Count Iblis is going to help us. Now relax. Come on, Apollo, dance with me."

"A wonderful idea," said Count Iblis. "Indeed, go on, Apollo. It will help you to get into the spirit of the occasion."

Sheba took Apollo's arm and led him onto the dance floor.

"They make a handsome pair," said Iblis.

Starbuck cocked an eyebrow at him.

"That's big of you," he said. "I kind of had the impression that you were interested in Sheba yourself."

"And why should she be limited to one man?" said Count Iblis. "Or you and I to one woman, for that matter?"

Starbuck grinned in spite of himself.

"Why do I get the feeling that I'd like this place you come from?" he said.

Count Iblis laughed and put his arm around Starbuck.

"Come, my friend, have a drink with me."

"Well, can't offend a guest," said Starbuck.

"More than a guest, Starbuck," said Count Iblis. "Soon to be your Lord."

Starbuck was about to reply with a sarcastic remark, but shrugged and decided to let it go. After all, what difference did it really make? If the man wanted to call himself a count or a lord, who was he to argue, so long as Iblis could produce results? Most of the people in the fleet seemed convinced of the fact that Count Iblis could lead them to Earth. If that were true, then they had a right to celebrate. And who was he to say that Iblis couldn't do it?

Count Iblis had done a lot of things that no one could explain. If he was half as powerful as he claimed to be, there was no reason in the world why he couldn't simply take control of the *Galactica* and of the fleet by force. Yet, he had not. He was content to let the people choose for

Battlestar Galactica 7

themselves. And if they chose to make him their lord, well, that was their decision.

Starbuck felt that he should be a lot more worried about Count Iblis than he was. Apollo clearly didn't trust the man, if man was what he was. What sort of man could make the trees in the Agro Ship suddenly bear fruit that was twice normal size and at least twice the normal yield? And *how* had he done it? Admittedly, he claimed to come from a race of beings far advanced beyond them. Starbuck knew that any technology that was sufficiently advanced would appear to be magic to the more primitive culture. If Count Iblis had such things to show them, to teach them, should he not rightfully become their "lord," if that was what the people wished?

He recalled how he had felt the first time he had seen the wreckage of the ship in which Count Iblis had traveled. It was impossibly huge, clearly created by a technology superior to theirs. If only they had been able to salvage some of its workings. . . .

It was difficult to think very clearly in the presence of Count Iblis. The man seemed to change from moment to moment. He could be warm, gracious, charming, his infectious smile could set anyone at ease. Yet Starbuck had also seen the arrogance in Count Iblis, the impatience, the danger. That was the key. Count Iblis was a dangerous man. Any man who could affect others as strongly as did Iblis was dangerous.

Starbuck accompanied Count Iblis to the bar. Two women came up and attached themselves to Iblis, who graciously "offered" one of them to Starbuck. She came around and took Starbuck's arm. The pilot noticed that her eyes were unfocused. She was much more than a little drunk.

Starbuck wondered if Count Iblis could get drunk. It was a good time to find out. There wasn't anyone in the fleet who was capable of drinking Starbuck under the table. Perhaps, thought Starbuck, the time had finally come to get some answers from Count Iblis. His way.

Starbuck smiled and raised his first glass in a toast.

A horrible sound woke him up. It faded in, as if from a dream into reality and through a thick haze of cotton it registered in Starbuck's mind as the red alert claxon blaring over the ship's p.a. system. He sat up, quickly. Too quickly. The room reeled before him and the vertiginous feeling was almost enough to make him vomit.

Starbuck clutched at his head, as if trying to squeeze it back into some semblance of its normal dimensions.

"Oh . . . my . . . *Lord*. . . ."

Reminding himself to move slowly, Starbuck glanced around at his surroundings. He was inside the ward room of the officer's quarters, lying on a bunk. He did not even remember coming back to the *Galactica*. In the center of the room, Boomer was lying half on and half off the meeting table, still in his full dress uniform. Obviously, he had mistaken the table for a bunk. He teetered on the edge of the table, threatening to fall onto the floor at any moment.

There were several other warriors in the ward room, which was not unusual, and there were several unconscious women there as well, which was. Some were slumped down in chairs, heads lolling grotesquely forward, others were stretched out in various attitudes upon the floor. And in various states of undress.

Apollo rushed into the ward room.

"Come on, come on, *what is this!*" He glanced about

him furiously.. *"This is a red alert!* Starbuck. . . ." He noticed his friend sitting, albeit unsteadily, on his bunk, trying to rub the crust out of his eyes. "Starbuck, come on, what's with you? Are you all right?"

Starbuck stared at Apollo and tried to remember how to make his mouth work. He couldn't seem to get any words out at all. It was as if someone's socks were wadded up inside his mouth.

"What in the . . ." Apollo leaned forward, peering intently into Starbuck's face. "Boomer. . . ."

At the sound of his name, Boomer jerked slightly and, overbalanced, crashed to the floor.

"Boomer! Get up, what's the matter with you?"

The din of the claxon finally penetrated Boomer's consciousness and he groaned, trying to stuff both fists into his ears in an effort to block out the sound.

"Starbuck," said Apollo, "where *is* everybody?"

"I don't think everyone made it back to the *Galactica,*" said Starbuck. His mouth was working, but the voice didn't sound like his. "That was some party."

"I don't believe it!" Apollo grabbed Starbuck by the shirtfront and pulled him out of the bunk. Starbuck hit the floor on his knees and the pain did a little to help wake him up. Then Apollo bent down and grabbed Boomer, shaking him.

A red alert, he thought furiously, and half the squadron is unaccounted for. And the ones who *are* here . . . aren't.

Adama came running onto the bridge. He stopped suddenly, looking around him. Colonel Tigh was at his station, but half of the bridge control consoles were unmanned.

"What is it?"

"More of those unidentified ships observing us," said

Tigh. "Or setting us up for whatever . . ."

"Still nothing on our scanners?" said Adama.

"Well, nothing on *my* scanner," Tigh said, wryly.

"Where *is* everyone?" Adama said, looking around at all the empty seats. "Colonel, what is the meaning of this?"

"A large number of our personnel are on life station relief," said Tigh.

"Has the Chief Life Officer been notified?"

"He, unfortunately, was one of the first stricken," Tigh said.

"What is it, a plague, a contamination?"

"No, sir," said Tigh. "Quite simply, it's an overdose of pleasure."

Adama scowled. "You can't be serious. What about the curfew for duty officers?"

Tigh shrugged. "Apparently some leeway was granted."

"By whom?"

"Count Iblis."

Adama looked out the massive observation window at the mysterious ships streaking past in all directions. It looked like the *Galactica* was caught in the midst of some strange energy shower. Adama's face was grim.

"I might have known," he said. "Launch a security screen at once. And have Count Iblis sent to my quarters immediately."

"Sir . . ." Tigh hesitated. "So far, no pilots have responded to the alert."

Adama was stunned. He turned to Tigh, an expression of shock and disbelief upon his face.

In the pilot's bay, Apollo was desperately trying to rally his squadron. Boomer kept sagging to the floor and Starbuck was struggling to get into his flight suit. Count Iblis entered and took in the situation at a glance.

"A disgraceful accounting of yourselves, gentlemen," he said. "The alert is fully twelve centons along and not a single ship has launched. Disgraceful, simply disgraceful—"

Unable to control himself, Apollo dropped Boomer and launched himself at Count Iblis, slamming into him and pinning him to the wall.

"Release me or forfeit your life," said Count Iblis. He started to raise a hand when Adama entered and called out to his son.

"Apollo! Have you lost complete control?"

Apollo spun around, releasing Count Iblis.

"You just saved your son's life," Count Iblis said. "Now, if this is your way to run a ship, Adama, I suggest we have more to take up with the council than my assuming the presidency. I may have to relieve you of command as military leader, as well."

He turned and walked rapidly toward the door, then hesitated and turned back to face the pilots once again.

"It appears to be of no interest to you young men," he said, "but the fleet is under attack. You, and you, and you . . ." he said, pointing to Apollo, Starbuck and Boomer, "had better respond to the claxon or I'll have you all in irons."

Adama stared at the three pilots, his fists clenched, his voice barely under control.

"Get to your ships," he said. *"At once."*

He turned his back on the pilots and hurried after Count Iblis, catching up to him in the corridor. He reached out and grabbed the count by the arm, holding him back. Iblis stared down at Adama's hand on his arm and Adama reluctantly released him.

"Who are they?" said Adama. *"What* are they? And what are *you?"*

Count Iblis stared at the commander coldly.

"I have told you all that you are capable of comprehending," he said. "Now don't interfere with me or you will regret it, I promise you."

Boomer looked at Starbuck and Apollo with pain written all over his face, but it was not the pain of a killer hangover. This was a pain that hurt far more than his head did, it was the pain of letting down his shipmates.

"I'm sorry, guys," he said thickly. "I *deserve* being put in irons for this kind of behavior. I just don't know what happened last night."

"I think I do," said Apollo. There was a hard edge to his voice.

"Don't bother explaining it to me right now," said Starbuck. "I'm having trouble finding my left eyelid."

"Can you fly?" Apollo said.

"We'll soon find out, won't we?"

They finished donning their flight suits and all but Apollo staggered to the cockpits of their Viper fighters. Starbuck strapped himself in, wondering why his hands felt like they belonged to someone else. Boomer kept fighting back nausea as he ran through his pre-flight check. It was taking them entirely too long.

Finally, urged on by Colonel Tigh's strident voice over their helmet comcircuits, the pilots launched their Vipers. The fierce acceleration of the sleek fighter craft as they hurtled down the launch tubes did much to clear the heads of the woozy fighter jocks, but they were still a long way from being one hundred percent as the Vipers cleared the tubes.

"Starbuck...straighten up your ship!" Apollo said urgently, seeing the shaky flight path taken by his wing man. "You're falling off formation!"

It was all Starbuck could do to keep the scanner in front of him from blurring.

"Falling off formation?" he said, still groggy from the festivities of the past few centons. "I'm falling off my seat. Must admit it's a first, though. I've never nodded out in combat before."

"Boomer, where in Hades' Hole do you think you're going?" Apollo said, watching with dismay as his other wing man separated from the formation and began to drift off.

"I got a bandit," Boomer slurred. "I've had it with these damn things. I'm going to get one of those white lights and make me a fireball..."

He zeroed in on one of the strange ships that dogged them and began firing his lasers. The moment he fired, the white light accelerated with dazzling speed, seeming to disappear. He never even came close.

"See *that?*" Boomer sounded triumphant, if a touch incoherent. "I blew that bandit right out of the universe! Nothing but space dust!"

"Boomer," Apollo said, worry edging his voice, "that ship left you standing still. Come on, man, wake up! Take your damn finger off the fire control before you overload your laser generator. You're not even giving it time to recycle!"

"Oh. Is it still on the trigger?"

"Boomer!"

"I . . . I think it's stuck," said Boomer.

"Your fire control?"

"No, my finger. . . ."

"Would you all please hold it down?" Starbuck's voice came over the comcircuit in a plaintive whine. "I've got a terrible cranial disturbance."

Apollo was exasperated. They were confronting ships that could outfly and outmaneuver them without any effort whatsoever and his squadron mates were dissociating with a vengeance.

"Look, you two—"

"Apollo, forget it," Starbuck said. "Look, they've all disappeared anyway. We can't catch 'em, whoever in hell they are. They're better than we are. I couldn't get a bead on those suckers even if my head wasn't falling off. . . ."

"And since Boomer shot at them," said Apollo, "they're liable to come back and attack the whole fleet."

"What for?" said Boomer. "I missed, didn't I?"

Starbuck began to giggle.

"I give up," said Apollo, disgustedly.

"Me, too," said Boomer.

"No, I mean I give up on you guys," Apollo said angrily. "You're nothing but a damn nuisance out here. You two return to the fleet. I assume you can find it. I'm going to continue on my own."

"Hey now," said Starbuck, a little more soberly, "I don't think that's such a good idea. One man out on—"

"That's an order, Starbuck," Apollo said. "Now you get Boomer back to the ship and get to the life station. You seem a little more aware of what's happening around you which, believe me, isn't saying much. So get him back there and get straightened out. I mean *now,* before he kills himself. Or one of us."

Apollo hit full power on his engines before either man had time to reply and raced off in the direction taken by the ship Boomer had fired upon.

Starbuck shook his head sadly, knowing that Apollo was right and feeling that he had let his friend down and, at the same time, knowing that it was stupid of him to continue on after those ships alone. However, he thought, given the speeds the mystery craft were capable of, there was little chance of Apollo's catching them.

He'll just fly around out here until he blows off steam, thought Starbuck. Then he'll come back to the ship and give me and Boomer holy hell. Which we'll deserve for acting like two duty-shirking rookies back from a furlough they couldn't handle.

"All right, Boomer," Starbuck said, "I think the man is right. Let's turn around and head back. Think you can make it?"

"Have I got a choice?"

"Not much of one. You could just float around out here for the rest of your life."

"I'm tempted, the way I'm feeling right now," said Boomer miserably.

"Come on," said Starbuck. "Just line up on me and I'll lead you in."

"Got ya."

Starbuck flipturned his Viper and worked out a course for the *Galactica,* tracking the battlestar on his scanner. He didn't notice that Boomer was beginning to fall behind.

Boomer leaned back against the cushion of his seat and shut his eyes, completely unaware that he was veering off course and losing Starbuck. It didn't seem to him as if he had any sleep at all. His eyelids were simply too heavy to force open.

It had been one hell of a party. And he had finally done it, had finally beaten Starbuck and Apollo.

He remembered Starbuck coming up to him in the locker room of the stadium, limping slightly. He had been furious.

"Man, Boomer, I know you wanted to win," Starbuck had said, "but that was *crazy* out there! Hell, you could have *killed* me that one time! What in God's name got into you?"

Starbuck had been very angry. Boomer had tried to think back to the game, to remember what it was he had done that had upset Starbuck so much, but he could not recall having done anything out of the ordinary. Certainly nothing that could have endangered Starbuck's life! He had simply played the best triad he knew how, as he had always done. Except he had won, for a change. Starbuck was just sore for having lost.

"Sour grapes," mumbled Boomer, feeling suddenly very drowsy.

The funny thing was, he couldn't remember very much about the game at all. He recalled telling Count Iblis how much he wanted to win, just once, just one damn time, and he remembered the strange way the count had looked at him, then hearing the ready call, taking his position on the line. . . .

The rest seemed a total blank.

It somehow figured that the one time he won, and a championship game, no less, he could not remember the finer moments of his victory. He wished he hadn't drunk quite so much.

How much *had* he drunk?

Boomer groaned, trying to force his eyes open. He had the feeling that there was something important he was supposed to be doing.

"*Man*, this is ridiculous," he mumbled. "I can hold my liquor better than that. . . ."

Count Iblis had congratulated him on his victory. He had seemed every bit as thrilled as he was, as if Iblis had played in the game himself. That was one thing Boomer remembered, the way Count Iblis had looked at him as he bought him drink after drink.

"His eyes shine," said Boomer. Then he began to chuckle. What *was* it he was supposed to be doing? Why couldn't he get his head sorted out?

He managed to open his eyes slightly, only to shut them instantly. The light hurt them, it was much too bright. He couldn't even see the scanner—

The scanner!

"Holy—" Boomer sat straight up, fear washing away the dullness that pervaded his entire body. "Asleep at the controls, for Kobol's sake! Space happy idiot, I—"

He couldn't see a single thing. His eyes were wide open, but everything around him was flooded with an intensely bright white light. Only once before had he experienced a similar phenomenon, back when he had been a cadet on leave, skiing the slopes of Mt. Ursus on Caprica. He had gone snow blind. Only this was worse. Much worse. The damn light *hurt*. Tears streamed from his eyes and his head began to ache even worse than it had before.

"Starbuck? Starbuck, where are you? You behind me?"

The light was so blinding that Boomer couldn't see that his scanner wasn't working. The comcircuit was dead as well, and the ship was out of control.

"Blue flight two to fleet," said Starbuck, keeping his eyes on the scanner to make sure he didn't botch the approach instructions. "Blue flight two to fleet, this is Starbuck requesting approach, repeat, Starbuck requesting approach. . . . I am leading Blue flight three in right behind me—"

"This is *Galactica* bridge control," Athena's voice came over Starbuck's comcircuit. "I have you on approach, Starbuck, but I don't have anyone else on my scanner. Where did you say Blue flight three was?"

Starbuck frowned. "Right behind me! He's right behind. . ."

Boomer wasn't there.

"Oh, *shit*. . . ."

Starbuck swung his ship around. Boomer was nowhere to be seen. He couldn't even read him on his scanner. Nor could he read the white light off in the distance. It wasn't on his scanner, but it was there.

"Boomer. . . ."

Boomer was beginning to panic. Something was coming up on him. Coming up *fast*.

"Starbuck? If that's you playing games, Starbuck, stop it, I can't stand it, I—"

It was directly overhead.

"Oh, my *God*. . . ."

The pain in his head became an unbearable agony. His hands left the useless controls and he grabbed his head, which felt as if it was being squeezed by some giant hand.

There was no time to scream.

CHAPTER SEVEN

"Look, it's my fault," said Starbuck softly. "I lost him."

Apollo shook his head. "No, I was responsible. Starbuck was in no condition to...well, that's not the point. I was in command. I never should have sent the two of them back—"

"Stop it, both of you," Adama said.

Both men fell silent. They were in Adama's quarters and the commander of the *Battlestar Galactica* leaned wearily against his desk. He looked like a much older man. Apollo was shocked at the strain that was evident in his father's face, in his whole bearing. Adama sighed.

"No one was in command," he said. "Just as no one is in command of this ship. Except maybe Count Iblis."

"What could he have to do with Boomer's disappearance?" said Apollo.

"What has he to do with anything?" Adama said. "Is he

making miracles? Or is he taking advantage of a race of beings he knows to be scrutinizing us?"

"He's one of them, that's what he is," said Starbuck.

"I don't know," Adama said. "These ships . . . or whatever they are have made no hostile move toward us."

"What do you call the disappearance of nine pilots?" said Apollo.

"We don't know that there is a connection," said Adama. "You've seen what they're capable of doing. Flying so fast that not even our scanners can pick up on them, surely they could have taken direct action against the ship by now if that was their intent. We seem to present no threat to them at all. We don't know for certain that there's a connection between our missing fighters and those strange ships. And if there is, what does it have to do with Count Iblis? Why?"

Apollo stared at his father. He had never seen Adama so indecisive before, so helpless. Ever since Count Iblis had come aboard, it seemed that Adama had been becoming more and more frustrated in his efforts to maintain command. He had been growing—Apollo hated to admit it— weaker. How was it possible for one man to have such an effect upon them all?

"I say we take him right back where we found him and dump him off," said Starbuck.

"I agree with you," Apollo said. "As you remember, I was against picking him up in the first place."

"I'm afraid the option of picking him up or not has passed," Adama said. "He has the complete support of every man, woman and child in the fleet. We couldn't lift a hand against him now if we wanted to. It would be inviting a revolution."

"Maybe," said Apollo. "And maybe not."

He turned and walked out of the room.

"Apollo," Adama called after him, "what are you going to do?"

There was no answer.

"I wouldn't worry about it," Starbuck said. He sounded bitter. "What can Apollo do, alone?"

It took a moment for the implication of what he said to sink in.

"I've got to go," said Starbuck.

The two pilots walked quickly down the corridor, heading toward the shuttle bay.

"I just want to remind you," Starbuck said, "this guy may not exactly warm the cockles of our hearts, but he seems to be capable of one mean bag of tricks."

"Maybe," said Apollo, "but I'm not so sure it isn't all coincidence."

"What do you mean?"

"I'm not exactly sure yet," said Apollo, "but something has been bothering me about Count Iblis. It's been eating away at me and I just can't seem to put my finger on it. One thing seems clear, though, and it's taken long enough, by God."

"And that is?" said Starbuck.

"And that is the fact that the major weapon in Count Iblis' arsenal seems to be ourselves."

"I don't follow you."

"Just stay with me, buddy," Apollo said, grimly. "Maybe I'm wrong, but this thing isn't over yet."

Four men walked slowly through the rows of trees on the Agro Ship. The old farmer moved with a lightness that belied his age and kept up a steady stream of conversation as he led Starbuck, Apollo, and Doctor Wilker through his domain. He could not seem to get over his amazement at the change in his orchard. He stared with wonder at each tree they passed, reaching out to touch the ripening fruit as if he could not believe that they were real.

"It's just like you see," he said, "bumper crops. Every single tree is producing like nothing I've ever seen. I'm telling you, it's a miracle. How else do you explain it?"

"What about that tree over there?" said Doctor Wilker, indicating a small tree in the center of the clearing. "That one over there doesn't look as if it's doing very well at all."

They approached it.

"Oh, yes, that one," said the farmer. "Now that is a little odd. I noticed that just a little while ago."

"What happened to it?" asked Wilker, examining the tree more closely.

"I can't tell you," the old farmer said in a puzzled voice. "It's a mystery to me. It was as healthy as could be a while ago. Last ship's day, it seemed to be doing fine. Not as well as all the others, but still. . . ."

"Curious," said Wilker. "It seems completely dead. And in so short a time. It doesn't make much sense."

"I'll tell you who might know," the old man said. "That miracle worker, Count Iblis. You should ask him."

"What does he have to do with it?" Apollo said.

The old man shrugged. "Well, he must have seen that there was something wrong with it even before I did. He was standing right next to it, where you are now."

"He was?" said Apollo. "What was he doing?"

"Did he touch it in any way?" said Starbuck.

"Well, I didn't want to be nosey, what with him and the girl carrying on and all, but yes, I think he did pull a leaf off, now that I recall. Sure enough, he did, right about there," the old man pointed.

Wilker shook his head. "I don't see how that could have anything to do with this bumper crop of food," he said. "I'd like to get back to the lab and do some more work on this, if it's all right with you, Captain."

"Let's go," said Apollo.

They arrived at the lab to find that Doctor Wilker had been examining several samples of all the fruit grown in the Agro Ship. They waited patiently, looking on as Wilker compared some of his previous findings to his observations of that day.

"You see here a sample of the fruit I have collected from the Agro Ship," said Wilker, indicating a pile on one of his lab tables, "and samples of other varieties we are growing in our hydrobeds, here."

"They look alike to me," said Starbuck.

"Yes, unusually large," said Wilker. "There is no question that they have responded to some extraordinary influence."

"Any ideas?" said Apollo.

"Possibly. Come over here."

Wilker led the two men over to several charts displayed on a bank of scanner monitors.

"Take a look right here," he said. "Our normal seismic and cosmic monitoring went right off the scale yesterday and today. According to calculations from the bridge, those occurrences coincided precisely with the presence of the unidentified ships, or flight of lights that encircled our fleet."

"In other words," Apollo said slowly, "those ships might have given off energy that could have influenced the growth of these plants."

"Could have," said Wilker. "It's possible. I mean, it's certainly no different in principle to plants leaning toward and receiving energy from a sun. It's only a theory, of course, and a half-baked one at that, but we don't know what sort of energy those white lights possessed. It's simply a matter of correlating two inexplicable phenomena. The timing's right."

"Then you think it was the white ships rather than Count Iblis that caused these plants to go crazy and grow like this?" said Starbuck.

"I said it's a possibility," said Wilker.

"I sure like it better than the alternative," Apollo said. "Thank you, Doctor. Keep on it."

They turned and left the lab together.

"Apollo," said Starbuck, "that look on your face. . . . What are you thinking?"

"Nothing," Apollo said. "Why don't you go rest up? You've had a pretty rough go of it lately. I want to do some thinking."

The fighter landing bay was dark and empty. The ground crews were off duty and only the sound of the force field generators broke the stillness of the cavernous chamber. The sound of the generators plus the soft hissing of the elevator as it arrived at the landing bay deck. The elevator door opened and, for a brief moment, a solitary figure was silhouetted in the light from inside. Then the door shut once again and the bay was once more plunged into darkness, with only the slight glow of several banks of red working lights giving a tiny amount of illumination.

Starbuck looked around, waiting a moment for his eyes to grow accustomed to the lack of light. Clutching a small pouch to his chest, he quickly sprinted across the bay, heading for a shuttle. He reached the shuttle hatch, stopped, looked around again and softly called out, "Apollo?"

Apollo stuck his head outside the shuttle hatch, saw Starbuck and quickly looked behind him, to see if he was alone.

"What are you doing here?" he said.

"I'm coming with you," Starbuck said, tapping his flight bag.

"No," Apollo said. "I thought we agreed on this. This is my gamble. I'm the only one who thinks there's something wrong with Count Iblis."

"You're the only one with guts enough to take him on," said Starbuck. "I'm coming with you and that's that. Now what's your plan?"

"Yes, I'd be interested in hearing that myself," said a voice from behind them.

The two pilots spun around, startled, to see Commander Adama standing in the shadows just behind them. Apollo glanced accusingly at Starbuck. The other pilot shrugged helplessly.

"I'm sorry," Starbuck said. "I was sure I wasn't followed."

"You weren't," Adama said, stepping up to them. "Boxey told me he saw Apollo slipping off with a flight bag. Well . . . let's hear it."

"Father, what I feel probably doesn't make any sense," Apollo said, "but I cannot put my faith into Count Iblis. I refuse to go along with everybody else."

"And why not?" said Adama. "He has done all that he promised, hasn't he?"

"Has he?" said Apollo. "Father, there are rational explanations for everything that's happened. The energy field projected by those mysterious ships or whatever they are. . . . Doctor Wilker feels that they could have spurred the growth of our food. Baltar's sudden appearance, as if in answer to Count Iblis' prophecy, I think it was simply a coincidence, another result of those unexplained lights. He was as frightened as we were."

"And what of Count Iblis' knowledge of Earth?" Adama said.

"That hasn't been proven."

"How can it be, until we allow him the chance to show us the way?"

"There is one more thing," said Apollo. "The ship, the one he claims to have come from."

"You saw the wreckage with your own eyes," said Adama.

"But we didn't examine it."

Adama frowned. "How could you have? The radion levels were dangerously high, isn't that what you reported?"

"Well, yes," said Starbuck. "I was handling the sensor. It reacted to the crash site, throwing off my readings. Count Iblis said that it was radion. I took his word for it."

"But if a people's intelligence has reached a state where they can move objects telekinetically . . ." said Adama.

Apollo nodded. "Maybe they can will sensors to react to nothing at all. That had occurred to me."

"What do you propose?" Adama said.

"I want to go back and examine the wreckage of that ship," Apollo said. "I want to see if I can find any evidence to verify the state of technology of that craft and its people. I want to be sure. It may not be much to go on, but I want very much to know why Count Iblis didn't want us going near that ship."

"And I want to go with him," Starbuck said.

"Because you also sense a deception?" said Adama.

Starbuck hesitated. "No. Because Apollo does. I'm half convinced that Count Iblis is everything he claims to be, but when it comes to following hunches, I'll put my life in Apollo's hands any day."

"Then go," Adama said.

"You don't object?" said Apollo.

"I had to play the devil's advocate," Adama said. "I wanted to be sure you two weren't going off half cocked. Officially, I cannot support you. But you're free men. If you don't choose to follow Count Iblis, that's your right."

Apollo sighed. "Thank you, Father. You understand, I would have cleared this with you first, except that—"

"You didn't want to put me into a position of having to say no. And then disobeying my orders, anyway." Adama smiled. "Now the only problem I have is avoiding the count. His abilities to pick up thoughtwaves could be dangerous to you."

Apollo nodded. "We'll try to get there and back before we're missed."

"God speed."

A short while later, on the bridge, a puzzled Colonel Tigh turned to Adama.

"Sir? A shuttle is requesting a launch. I don't seem to

have any missions scheduled and there have been no advance requests for interfleet shuttles. Captain Apollo said to check with you."

"Oh, yes, Colonel," said Adama, "my fault. I neglected to check with you when I gave them clearance. One of the passenger ships requested some firsthand instruction in triad for some of the children. Apollo thought it would be wise to have some experienced players conduct the lessons, since it could be somewhat dangerous, even with the modified rules for the youngsters. Besides, I thought that it would impress the children to have some real champions come out to teach them."

"A nice idea," said Tigh.

Adama smiled and nodded, then turned to leave the bridge. He hesitated a moment.

"Oh, by the way," he said to Tigh, "you wouldn't happen to know the whereabouts of Count Iblis at this moment, would you, Colonel?"

"Yes," said Tigh, "I believe he's visiting the Agro Ship. With Sheba, if I'm not mistaken. I remember giving clearance to the shuttle."

"Ah. If he should ask to see me, would you convey my apologies? I'm bone weary and I must take a sleep period."

"For how long, sir?"

"Until further notice. I'm sure you can handle things for a while."

"Thank you, Commander. Have a good rest."

Adama left the bridge, en route to his private quarters. Tigh went back to his post, checked the scanners and frowned slightly.

"Athena," he said, "the shuttle just launched. Have they

communicated their docking instructions with one of the passenger ships?"

"Passenger ships?" said Athena, checking her monitor. "I don't think I follow you, Colonel. This doesn't seem to be an interfleet flight. Shuttle Alpha just headed off away from the fleet."

"*Away* from the fleet?"

"Yes, Colonel. Is something wrong?" Athena said.

"No, no, probably not. What could be wrong? I must have misunderstood. . . ."

Tigh thought for a moment. He was certain that the commander had told him that Apollo was going on a short interfleet hop, but then if the shuttle was heading *away* from the fleet. . . . He shrugged. Apollo knew what he was doing. If there was any trouble, he would most certainly have communicated with the bridge. The commander's son was a stickler for doing things by the book. Perhaps he was using the flight as an opportunity to check himself out on the shuttles once again. There was no telling when a Cylon attack might catch a pilot in an undefended vehicle. A good pilot made certain that he was always in practice, able to execute complicated evasive maneuvers and such. Of course, that had to be it. Apollo would want to put the shuttle through its paces well away from the fleet. And it was just like him to kill two birds with one stone, combining a routine flight with a practice flight. Tigh ceased to concern himself with the matter.

Sheba stretched out on the ground next to Count Iblis. He put his arm around her shoulders and she nestled her head against his chest. She felt relaxed and completely at peace with herself and with the world around her, the world that was an artificial forest, enclosed by cold metal. Yet, on the Argo Ship, it was possible to forget that she was a refugee without a world to go home to. It was possible to pretend, at least for a little while, that she was lying on a green carpet of moss, staring up at the starlit sky of Caprica.

"It's so beautiful here," she said softly.

"Yes," Count Iblis said, smiling. "It is a garden, a veritable paradise."

"It's the only place that comes close to what we lost," said Sheba. "Even if it's drifting through space, it's alive. You can feel it."

Iblis suddenly stiffened. The smile vanished from his face. He sat up, quickly, dislodging Sheba.

"What is it?" she said.

Count Iblis stared up at the dome, out at the stars.

"What are you up to?" he said.

"What?" said Sheba. "I wasn't doing any—"

Count Iblis rolled to his feet and quickly hurried away from her, moving toward the shuttle bay.

"Wait!" said Sheba, starting after him, a confused expression on her face. "Where are you going? What's the matter?"

She barely managed to catch up to him, but no matter what she said, she could not break through to him. All the way back to the *Galactica,* he ignored her questions. He sat very still, bolt upright, his hands clenching and unclenching on his knees, a faraway look in his eyes, a look of fury on his face. Sheba could not imagine what had happened. What had she said to offend him? Perhaps he wasn't feeling well? What? He would not respond. When the shuttle docked with the *Galactica,* he was out the hatch in a flash, running down the corridor. She could not keep up.

On the bridge, Tigh stood by his scanner.

"Athena, do we have a progress report on Shuttle Alpha?" he said.

"It is just leaving scanner range, Colonel," she said.

"Leaving scanner range? But that makes no sense whatsoever. Why would they do that? What is their course?"

"Heading toward the planet where—"

"Where my ship crashed," said Count Iblis, coldly.

Tigh jerked, startled by Count Iblis' sudden arrival.

"Count Iblis! Where did you come from? I didn't hear you walk—"

"Who is in that shuttle?" Iblis said, his voice like ice.

"I don't know, exactly," Tigh said, wary of Iblis' tone.

"Captain Apollo and who else?" said Iblis, his eyes blazing.

"I really don't know, I—"

"Where is Adama?"

"Well, he's—"

"Thank you, Colonel."

Iblis turned and left the bridge. Tigh hurried over to his communicator. Microns later, Commander Adama's face appeared on the screen.

"Yes, Colonel? What is it?" said Adama.

"I'm sorry, sir, but it's Count Iblis. I think he's on his way to see you. And I believe it has something to do with the shuttle you cleared for—"

Adama stiffened. "Thank you, Colonel. I'll handle it."

No sooner had Tigh's image disappeared off the screen than the door to Adama's cabin opened and Count Iblis walked in.

"I was under the impression that the door was secured," said Adama.

Iblis ignored the remark. "You gave your word that you would follow me," he said.

"How have we broken our word?" Adama said.

"You have sent your son in search of my identity."

Adama met his stare.

"I thought you told us your identity, Count Iblis," he said evenly.

"Don't play games with me," said Iblis. "When a mortal breaks a bargain with me, there is a high price to be paid."

"Then take your toll on me, Iblis. I have done what I had to do. The people in the fleet are *my* responsibility."

"No, Adama," Count Iblis said. "Forfeiting your life would be too easy. And too little. There is a greater price that you will pay."

Count Iblis spun around and walked out the door. Adama paled when he realized just what that price would be. And suddenly, he knew, without a shadow of a doubt, that Count Iblis could exact it.

"No, wait! I beg of you, take me. . . ."

He rushed out into the corridor. He looked both ways. There was no sign of Count Iblis. Adama sagged against the bulkhead. Sheba came running down the corridor, trying to catch Count Iblis. She stopped when she saw Adama, who appeared to be on the verge of tears.

"Adama! *What is it?*"

"We have sold our souls to a demon," said Adama in a broken voice.

"What are you talking about?"

"Count Iblis," said Adama.

Sheba smiled. "Why can't you understand?" she said. "He only means what's best for us. Why don't you trust him? He is the answer to all our prayers! Our deliverer. . . ."

"Tell that to my son," Adama said. "And Starbuck."

Sheba stared at him, not understanding.

"Why?" she said. "What have they done? Where are they?"

"They have gone to prove Count Iblis for what he really is," Adama said. "God help them."

"Why?" said Sheba. "I don't understand. What could Count Iblis—"

"Commander!" Tigh came running down the hall from the opposite side. "Are you all right?"

"Did you tell Count Iblis where Starbuck and Apollo went?" Adama said.

"I didn't tell him anything about the shuttle, Commander," Tigh said, "but he knew."

"Did you pass him in the corridor?" Adama said, already knowing, fearing what the answer would be.

"No."

"Is he still on board?"

"So far as I know," said Tigh. "Nothing else has launched toward the planet where we found his ship."

"So that's where they've gone!" said Sheba. "Those fools! All of you, *fools!* Don't you know what you've done? We gave him our word!"

"Sheba, you don't see what he—"

"I only see that you've ruined everything!" she shouted. "All he ever wanted to do was help us! And now you've . . . you've. . . ."

She couldn't finish. With a look of hatred, she turned

and ran back down the corridor, heading for the launch bay.

"Sheba!" Tigh started after her, but Adama held him back.

"Let her go," Adama said. "She's too blinded by Count Iblis to listen to reason. Quickly, Tigh, we must find him, we have to stop him somehow."

"I don't think I understand," said Tigh.

"That's because it's almost incomprehensible," Adama said.

They ran to the bridge together. Once there, every scanner, every communicator was used in an effort to track down Count Iblis, but Adama was almost certain that they would not find him. They communicated with each and every deck of the battlestar, quickly organized search parties, but it was to no avail. It was as if Iblis had disappeared without a trace.

"No sign of Count Iblis on any of the decks, Commander," Tigh said, checking with the search parties throughout the battlestar.

"And nothing from any of the other ships in the fleet," said Rigel. "No one has seen him. Absolutely no one. How is that possible?"

"If he were anywhere on the *Galactica,* or on any of the ships within the fleet, we'd know it," Tigh said.

"There is one possibility," Athena said. "A single Viper launched without a clearance just a little while ago."

"Sorry," Tigh said. "That was Sheba."

"Sheba?" said Adama. "Then she's gone after them."

Tigh nodded. "The ground crews in the launch bay confirmed it. They tried to stop her, but. . . ." His voice trailed off and he spread his arms out from his sides in a gesture of resignation. "Evidently she got a little violent with some of them and, well, you know Sheba. I'd hesitate to get in her way if she didn't want to be stopped."

"Father," said Athena, looking up from her console, "you're going to have to make some sort of statement. All the comcircuits are jammed. Our search has word spreading throughout the fleet. They want to know what happened."

"She's right," said Tigh. "For Count Iblis to simply disappear like that, I mean, we've got to find him. He has to be here someplace. There must be someplace that we've overlooked."

"No," said Adama, sinking down into his chair. "We won't find him."

"But how can we explain that?" said Athena.

"We can't," Adama said. He leaned forward and put his head in his hands. For a long while, he didn't speak and everyone on the bridge stared at him anxiously.

"Commander?" Tigh said, finally.

Adama did not respond.

CHAPTER EIGHT

Everything around them was the color of dried blood. Starbuck and Apollo moved up the hill of red grass, having landed their shuttle at the base of the crater. They had spotted the wreckage of the giant ship from the air, as they had before. Nothing had changed. Only this time, nothing would prevent them from descending down to the ship. They reached the crest and looked down.

Even though they had seen it once before, the size of the wrecked ship astounded them. It made them feel like insects. Next to the wrecked ship, the *Galactica,* a ship of the battlestar class, the largest craft ever built by humans, would appear to be little more than the size of a Viper fighter. It was awesome and it was frightening. Even more so now that they knew something of the nature of the beings that had flown it. But they didn't know enough.

"That's where the answer lies," Apollo said. "If there *is* an answer."

Starbuck smiled weakly. "I'm not even sure I understand the question."

"Let's go," said Apollo.

They started down the hill toward the wreckage, holding their sensors out before them.

"Nothing," Starbuck said.

"I knew it," said Apollo. "The radion danger was a myth. Iblis manipulated our sensor readings somehow."

"How is that possible?" said Starbuck. "I mean, telekinesis is one thing, but. . . ."

"How is anything Count Iblis does possible?" Apollo said. "He did it, that's all that concerns me right now. Let's go have a look at her crew."

They entered the wreckage.

Sheba arrived in time to see them go into the ship's carcass. She started to cry out to them, then thought better of it. She ran down the hill, almost losing her footing several times. She wasn't even sure why she had come.

What was the point of it all? What could they possibly hope to accomplish, except to prove to Count Iblis that they were not worthy of his trust. As her Viper fighter had raced toward the red planet, she had tried desperately to sort out her thoughts and feelings. She couldn't seem to think clearly. All she knew was that she loved Count Iblis. She had never met anyone like him before. There was an aura about him that was incredibly compelling. She could not resist him and she didn't want to. He was more than a mere man. He hadn't lied to them about that. Hadn't he told them all that he was from a race that was far advanced beyond theirs?

He had proved his power and he had proved his good intentions. He wanted only to help them all and he had left the choice up to them. He had created miracles, caused their food to grow better than ever before, brought them Baltar, humbled before the council. What more could they possibly want? He even promised to show them the way to Earth. He could do all those things and more. Wasn't it right, then, that he should lead them? Was it so much to ask?

Apollo climbed over the wreckage of a toppled bank of instruments. Everything inside the ship, or what was left of it, was on a massive scale.

"It's all pretty well vaporized," he said, shaking his head with wonder. "God, whatever hit this thing must have had the power of a sun! I can't even begin to imagine what—"

He froze.

"Starbuck!"

"What is it? What did you find?"

"Come over here and give me a hand."

Apollo started to put on some protective gauntlets. Starbuck came up beside him, glanced at him, then looked down at what Apollo had seen.

Something was pinned beneath a giant piece of metal, part of the bulkhead which had collapsed. It was a body. The only visible part of the body was the lower leg, sticking out from underneath the wreckage.

The leg ended in a cloven hoof.

"What in hell is *that?*" said Starbuck.

"Strange that you should say that," said Apollo. "I'm about to find out just what in hell it is. But unless my imagination is working overtime, I'm afraid that I already have a pretty good idea."

He bent down and grasped the slab of metal, trying to lift it. It was too heavy. Starbuck slipped on a pair of gauntlets and joined him. Together, they strained and managed to lift the wreckage, tossing it aside.

The body underneath was shattered and burned, but its form was recognizable. It was large, twice as large as a human. It had a head, two arms and two legs, but there any resemblance to human form ended. Its torso, although flattened by the piece of metal that had fallen upon it, was grotesquely large and misshapen. The chest cavity was huge. The fingers ended in talons and there were horns upon its head, sprouting from just above the eyes, which insects had eaten away. The body was in an advanced state of decomposition and the smell was overpowering. In spite of it, both men were rooted to the spot. The thing had hooves. And a long, prehensile tail.

"Starbuck! Apollo! What are you doing?"

Sheba stood just inside the shattered hull of the ship. She started to move toward them.

"Sheba, stay back!" said Starbuck.

"I won't stay back. What is it you've found?"

Apollo grabbed her and started to push her back, trying to force her back outside. She struggled against him.

"Let go of me!"

"Sheba, believe me," said Apollo, "you don't want to go in there."

"I want to see."

"Apollo," Starbuck said softly, "maybe she should."

Sheba stopped struggling.

Apollo nodded, letting her go. "Maybe you're right."

"I don't know what you're trying to prove here," Sheba

said, "but I want you to know that nothing will change my mind about Count Iblis."

"Go take a look," Apollo said.

She looked at him defiantly. "All right. I will."

She started to step forward.

"No!"

Through the rupture in the ship's hull, they could see Count Iblis standing on the crest of the hill, his robes billowing about him in the wind. He stretched forth his hands and energy crackled. He threw his hands up and lightning seemed to shoot down from the sky and bathe him in fire. There was a deafening clap of thunder.

"I forbid it!"

His voice sounded almost as loud as the thunder. Starbuck and Apollo both reached for their sidearms, resting their hands on the butts of their laser pistols.

Iblis beckoned to Sheba.

"Sheba, come away from there. Come to me," he said.

Apollo glanced at Sheba. She was staring up at Count Iblis. Her eyes were wide and glazed. Her lips were trembling. There was a vacant look upon her face, a look Apollo had seen once before. It was the same look he had seen on Boomer's face during the triad game.

Apollo reached out and grasped Sheba's arm. "Don't listen to him, Sheba. Don't look at him. Turn around and take a look at what Starbuck and I found. You said you wanted to see, didn't you? Well, *look,* Sheba! Go see for yourself! It's what you wanted!"

"Don't be deceived, child," Iblis called down to her. "You are mine. Come be with me."

Slowly, Sheba began to move forward. Apollo tried to

hold her back, but she shook his arm off.

"Sheba!" Starbuck shouted. "Sheba, turn around!"

Apollo lunged for her.

"Do not touch her!" Iblis said. "She is mine. She has given herself freely."

Apollo grabbed her and spun her around. She looked right through him.

"Sheba! Please, snap out of it! Hear me...."

"Let go of her," Count Iblis said. "I command it!"

Apollo swung on him furiously.

"You command no one who doesn't willingly give you dominion. You have no power over me."

"So you know who I am," Count Iblis said.

"Yes. I finally know." Apollo turned to Sheba, shaking her. "Think, Sheba! Think back to the ancient records, the Book of Kobol—"

"I can't," she said, cutting him off. "Apollo, you don't understand, you're wrong about him. Count Iblis—"

"No, Sheba, not Count Iblis," said Apollo. "The name's Diabolis. The Prince of Darkness."

"I warned you not to interfere," Count Iblis said. "I'll give you one last chance to step away or I will strike her down."

Count Iblis raised his hand and at that moment Apollo pulled his laser pistol and fired at him. The energy beam lanced out at him and bathed him in a wash of light. His features seemed to change. For an instant, it wasn't Count Iblis who stood upon the crest, but another sort of creature entirely, one that did not look human. The creature laughed, unhurt.

"You have brought her death, Apollo," it said. "And may her lost soul curse you throughout eternity!"

The air crackled with electricity and lightning crashed down on the crest. Iblis reached up, seeming to draw power from the lightning. Apollo jumped in front of Sheba, throwing her to one side. In so doing, he caught the full force of the energy blast thrown by Count Iblis. He stiffened as the brilliant aura surrounded him, then sank slowly to the ground.

Starbuck watched with shocked disbelief as his friend crumpled to the ground. It had all happened so fast that he hadn't even had a chance to move. The sight of Apollo sheathed in that deadly halo of energy stunned him momentarily. He could not believe that his friend was dead.

"*Apollo!*" he screamed, rushing over to the spot where he had fallen. He bent down and lifted Apollo's head from the ground. Apollo was limp. There was no breath, no heartbeat.

"He's dead," Starbuck said. He looked up at Count Iblis, Diabolis, the creature who had masqueraded as a human. "You killed him!"

Starbuck aimed his laser pistol at Diabolis and fired again and again, barely giving the weapon an opportunity to recycle. Diabolis stood upon the crest of the ridge, laughing as the bolts of energy struck him repeatedly, without effect. Starbuck lowered his weapon, feeling an impotent, helpless rage. His best friend had been killed by a creature against whom he was powerless. It occurred to him that he would undoubtedly be next. He didn't care.

Diabolis stretched forth his hand to Sheba, beckoning to her.

"Come, Sheba," he said.

She got up slowly from the ground, staring at Diabolis and seeing his true nature for the first time. As if in a trance, she moved toward Starbuck, kneeling by the fallen body of Apollo.

"Sheba!"

She stared up at Diabolis with loathing.

"No," she said.

"Sheba, you belong to me," said Diabolis. "You freely gave yourself to me. You want to come with me, you—"

"No!" she shouted. "No, I could never follow you! Apollo! What have I done?"

She began to cry hysterically. Starbuck stood up and took her in his arms, attempting to calm her. There was nothing more that he could do. The strongest weapon he possessed had no effect upon the creature who had called itself Count Iblis. His fate was no longer of concern to him. The creature had to kill them now. It didn't matter. There was nothing they could do, except one thing. They could show him that they were not afraid.

"It wasn't your fault, Sheba," Starbuck told her. "You didn't do it. He did it, Diabolis, or whatever his name really is."

He looked up at the creature standing on the ridge.

"It's over, isn't it? Your power over us is finished. You can't force us to follow you. We had to be willing."

"Yes, that is true," said Diabolis. "I cannot force your obedience. But I can destroy you."

A strange, high-pitched whining sound filled the sky. Diabolis looked up, startled. Countless bolts of white hot light screamed across the sky above them. Diabolis turned pale. He stared up at the sky with fear.

The strange white ships were back. They came down in formation, flying low over the ground, but so fast that it was impossible for Sheba and Starbuck to make out any details of their construction. Like laser beams, they shot by overhead with incredible speed.

"What is it, Diabolis?" called Starbuck, over the keening wail of the ships passing overhead. "What's wrong?"

"Nothing is wrong!" Diabolis screamed back, furiously.

"Then why do you look so worried? You're the one with all the power! Or did you overstep your bounds? Did you break some kind of rule, Diabolis?"

"There are no rules! No one has dominion over me!"

"I wonder," Sheba said. "In all the universe, are there not balances? Rules, even for an advanced race, a greater law?"

The white lights swept back over them again. There seemed to be more of them than there were on their first pass.

"I am not finished with you mortals," Diabolis said. "There will be another time and another place. We will meet again."

He threw his arms out to his sides and the air around him crackled with energy, then the sky over the ridge became filled with light, a bright glowing light like that of a sun going nova. Starbuck and Sheba turned away, shielding their eyes against the blinding light. An explosion shook the air and ground around them, tumbling them to the earth. When they looked up, Diabolis was gone. The sky was clear and there was no sign of the mysterious white ships. Everything was still around them.

Sheba scanned the ridge, searching for any sign of Diabolis. They were alone.

"Starbuck," she said, "he just vanished! Everything is as it was when he first appeared."

"No," Starbuck said softly, looking down at the inert

form of Apollo. "One thing is different. Let's take him home."

Together, they picked up Apollo and carried him back to the shuttle. They strapped his body down and lifted off, leaving the red planet behind them. They did not look back.

FROM THE ADAMA JOURNALS:

There have been many times during my life when I have
felt afraid. A man who never feels fear is either a fool or
he is insane. I have known fear in times of combat, both
when I was young and inexperienced in the ways of warfare
and when I was a senior officer, my rank making me responsible for the lives of those warriors under my command.
The latter is the greater fear by far, for it is an easy thing
to lay one's own life upon the line. Even a man who is an
abject coward can experience a moment when life and death
no longer seem to matter. We all have our limits of endur-
ance and when those limits are reached, we all react in
different ways.

Often, there is nothing "heroic" in a hero. I cannot count
the times that I have seen warriors who hungered for glory
throw their lives away in foolish actions they perceived as
being heroic. Heroes are neither born nor made. Most often,
they become heroes by accident.

Such was the case with me. When I was a child, I had dreams of glory. Those dreams persisted through my adolescence and they stayed with me through my training at the academy. My people were at war with an enemy dedicated to the complete extermination of the human race. I hated the Cylons and it was easy for me to picture myself as a Viper fighter pilot, defending Caprica from the alien menace. I set myself a goal. I would be more than just a warrior, a Viper fighter pilot. I would be an avenger, killing more Cylons than any other warrior, winning recognition as a soldier who would take any risk to save his people. I would be a hero. A Viper ace. Foolish, foolish dreams. How quickly they evaporated the first time I saw combat.

I still remember, vividly, my first launch into combat with the Cylons. I was ready. I was filled with a self-righteous rage. I could not wait to get my first Cylon fighter in my sights and blow the enemy to space dust. And, the first time that it happened, it was easy. It took no great skill on my part, merely luck. I fired my lasers and scored my first kill in my very first time out in combat. I felt exhilarated. I felt proud. I felt indestructible. And microns later, I felt the cold fist of fear squeezing my insides as I was caught in a Cylon pinwheel attack.

In that one moment, all my dreams of glory faded. Only one thing mattered. Staying alive. In that one moment, the fact of my own mortality was brought home to me in the most direct way possible. I was hemmed in by the enemy and they were trying to kill me. I was not a hero then. I wept with fear. The other members of my squadron saved me from what seemed to me a certain death and from that time on, the war was not the same for me. I realized then, for the first time, that I was not a hero. I was no avenger.

I only wanted to survive. It was only then that I finally understood what the war, and what life, was all about.

Survival.

I stopped taking chances, stopped gambling with my life. I had found out just how much it meant to me. I became the most cautious and conservative of pilots, not out of any sense of wisdom, but out of fear. It was quite simple. I knew I had to fight. And I did not want to die.

It sounds absurd. Of course, no sane person wants to die. But life takes on a different aspect when every day is lived with just one goal in mind—avoiding death.

For a long time, I thought myself a coward. I kept to myself, avoiding the company of the other pilots. They thought me aloof, but in fact, I did not feel that I was worthy of their friendship. I was afraid to die and it was our job to face death. I began to do everything "by the book." I avoided taking risks as much as possible. And every time my Viper hurtled down the launch tube, I prayed to God to let me live. I felt ashamed of what I was. And then something happened that was to change my life forever. It was, of course, an accident.

It happened during the Battle of Sagittaria. Our forces were caught in a Cylon ambush and we were badly outnumbered. I was assigned to the Bronze squadron of the *Battlestar Cerebrus.* My wing mates were Lieutenant Cain, who was later to command the *Pegasus,* and Lieutenant Apollo. Yahrens later, when my son was born, I named him in honor of my friend.

Lieutenant Apollo was little more than a boy. Seventeen yahrens old, he had graduated from the academy at the age of sixteen, the youngest cadet ever to win his commission. Apollo was a brilliant boy; he had breezed through the academy in a mere two yahrens. The youngest to be admitted and the youngest to graduate. Only Cain, who graduated at the head of his class, scored higher marks. Apollo graduated number two and I was number three. We became inseparable and it was only fitting that we be assigned to the same squadron in the *Cerebrus,* the ship we had requested.

Everybody loved Apollo. His charm and ready wit won him friends everywhere he went. He was an incorruptible innocent whose lust for life infected everyone around him. He was the only one in whom I could confide, though he was younger than I. Not even Cain knew of my fear, my cowardice. Indeed, Cain would not have understood.

Cain was, in very many ways, like Starbuck. Even then, we knew that Cain was destined for command, for heroism. Cain was what many people called a "war lover." It is a term used by those who simply cannot understand. Most often those who use it have never been in combat. It was not that Cain loved war, loved killing, loved taking risks, rather it was that Cain really only lived when he was on the razor's edge. He was aware of the danger. He understood it well and thrived on it.

Apollo, on the other hand, never seemed to understand it. The fantasy that left me when I first went into combat stayed with him. Apollo genuinely believed that he could not be hurt. He had a hopelessly naive, yet charming belief that since right was on his side, he would prevail. We would talk late into the night, he trying to help me see that my fear was what was ruling me and preventing me from having happiness, I trying to convince him that he would get himself killed taking foolhardy risks. Neither of us ever convinced the other.

He saved my life during the Battle of Sagittaria. I became separated from the squadron and suddenly found myself with three Cylon fighters on my tail. I could not elude them. I knew that I would die. Apollo came from out of nowhere, having left the safety of the squadron formation to save my hide. He accounted for two of the fighters on my tail, but as I continued trying to elude the third, Apollo found himself caught in a devastating Cylon pinwheel attack. I could not break away to help him. The other pilots in the squadron were too busy trying to stay alive themselves. There was no one to save him, as he had saved me.

I can still remember his last words to me as his voice came over my helmet comcircuit. I can still hear the surprise in his voice as he realized that he was mortal after all, despite the fact that right was on his side.

"My God, I'm dead," he said. "Remember me, Adama."

Then there was a blinding flash of light and Apollo was no more.

Since that time, again and again I've wondered what came over me. At the time, I did not know. Looking back now, with the wisdom gained over the yahrens, I can understand what happened. It was an accident, the sort of accident that gives birth to heroes.

Before Apollo came to my assistance, I had resigned myself to the fact that I was going to die. I could not shake those Cylon fighters on my tail. I was using everything I knew to maintain evasive action, but I knew that it was only a matter of microns before one of the searing beams of light that kept flashing past my ship would score a direct hit and I would die, incinerated in a blazing fireball. I realized that it would happen quickly, too quickly for me to feel anything, probably too quickly for me to even realize that it had happened. I realized all that and my fear just went away. It simply didn't matter any more. A strange calm came over me and, with it, an acceptence of my fate.

Only, it was not to be. The fate that had been mine became Apollo's. He took it from me. I had prepared myself for death and suddenly was confronted with the fact that I would live, at least for a little while more. The fear did not return. After all, in a way, I had already died. There was no point to being afraid of something that had already happened.

The rest of what happened during the battle is not clear in my memory. I recall somehow disposing of the Cylon fighter on my tail and single-handedly attacking the ships that had destroyed Apollo. It was the action of a lunatic, perhaps, or the final struggles of a man who was already dead but had yet to stop moving. I remember Cain taking up position on my wing as we ploughed straight through the Cylon formation, two ships heading alone directly for the Cylon base ship. I don't remember very much of what happened after that.

The squadrons rallied round us and the tide was turned, Cain and I were heroes. Both of us won our promotions, becoming captains. Both of us were placed on the paths which would lead to our commanding our own battlestars. Cain would command the *Pegasus* and I, the newly commissioned *Galactica*. But that was in the future. At the celebration following the battle, in the officer's lounge aboard the *Cerebrus,* there was much drinking and much laughter and much talk of bravery, of mine and Cain's. I did not disillusion them. There was no point to it and, besides, I did not know how to tell them what had really happened. Yet, I remember the way Cain looked at me during the feast. He knew. He never mentioned it, to me or anybody else, but he knew.

As I speak these words, here alone in my private quarters on the *Galactica,* I wonder how Cain would look at me right now. I wonder what he would have done and I think back to the time when the man—a very young man, but a man nevertheless—for whom my son was named was still alive.

How different they are, the two Apollos. My friend and my son. Lieutenant Apollo was rash, impetuous, playful and energetic. My son is far more reserved, cool, some think him cold, though I know better, always in control. Yet, there is one thing that my son has in common with the man whose name he bears. The belief that right and goodness will prevail. It was that belief which killed my friend, and now I fear that it has claimed my son, as well.

Am I still a coward, then? Was I wrong not to take on Count Iblis from the beginning? Did I send my own son to his death when I gave him and Starbuck my approval to go on their mission? Why did I not act when I had the chance? Or would it have made no difference?

A clever man, Count Iblis. No, not a man, Something else, something horrible. He played on all our fears, all our insecurities, all our hopes and dreams. Perhaps I could have stopped him. Perhaps he is too strong and nothing I could have done would have prevented him from accomplishing his goal. I do not know. I should have tried. I should have done *something*.

My people wait for me. I am the commander, it is my duty to provide the answers, to give them leadership. Yet, I have no answers and I have not the heart to lead. Count Iblis has disappeared and everyone within the fleet is clamoring to know where he has gone. They are afraid that they have lost their saviour, the man who shows them miracles and will lead them all to Earth. What can I tell them?

Do I tell them, have no fear, your saviour will return? He has only gone to kill my son.

CHAPTER NINE

Starbuck sat at the controls of the shuttle, staring straight ahead. He seemed to be almost in a fugue state, there was a lifelessness about him, a mechanical aspect to his motions. Sheba sat beside him, tears rolling down her cheeks. Behind them, his lifeless body strapped down tightly, was Apollo.

"I'm sorry," Sheba kept saying over and over again, an endless litany, "it was all my fault."

"No," said Starbuck. His voice was flat and dull, emotionless. "You were not alone. It seems to me that everyone was trying to find someone or something to believe in."

"Apollo knew better," Sheba said softly. "Why did he have to be the one to pay?"

Starbuck shook his head. "I don't know the answer to that," he said. "All I know is that I'd gladly trade my life to get him back."

Something flashed by their shuttle, traveling at an astonishing speed.

"Starbuck?" Sheba said.

"I see them."

The swarm of lights hurtled past their shuttle as if it was hanging dead in space. They sped out in front of them, then, still grouped together, arced back and came toward them once again. They came at the shuttle with blinding speed, flashed past them and came back again.

"Here we go again," said Starbuck bitterly. "As if we haven't been through enough."

Sheba reached out and took his hand, holding onto him with desperation.

"What *are* they, Starbuck? What do they mean? What do they want from us?"

Starbuck shook his head. "I don't know. Whatever they are, there's nothing we can do against them. The shuttle isn't armed and we can't maneuver like a Viper. And even a Viper is no match for their speed."

"If only I hadn't left my fighter back on that planet," Sheba said, "I could have—"

"You could have done nothing," Starbuck told her. "I've tried chasing these things in a Viper. It's impossible. Whatever they are, they're just too damned fast. Besides, you're in no shape to fly. We'll send someone back for your Viper. That is, of course, assuming we'll get back."

The lights flew by them once again, moving so quickly that they seemed to trail streamers of dazzling brilliance behind them like the tails of comets. Starbuck's hands tensed on the shuttle's controls. Once again, the swarm of white lights sped out a distance ahead of them, then arced back, up and out of sight. Starbuck and Sheba sat for a while in tense silence. The lights did not come back. Starbuck sighed, visibly relieved.

"Whatever it means," he said, "whatever they are, they're gone. At least for now. See if you can compute the range back to the fleet."

Sheba nodded and bent forward over the control console of the shuttle. She had difficulty seeing the screen. It seemed much too bright. Then she noticed that it wasn't the screen that was too bright. The entire cockpit of the shuttle was bathed in a wash of blinding light. It grew brighter and brighter until she could no longer see. She squinted, her eyes tearing from the glare.

"Starbuck, what is it? What's happening, where is it coming from?"

"I don't know what it is," said Starbuck, attempting to shield his eyes from the glare with one hand. "It's coming from above and behind us. See if you can get a look at—"

Starbuck's head jerked back and his hands left the controls to clutch at the sides of his head.

"Starbuck!" Sheba cried. "The pain, I can't stand it!"

Fighting back the pain, Starbuck forced his hands back down onto the controls of the shuttle. They were under some sort of an attack, but from what, neither of them knew. All Starbuck felt was the agony of an incredible pressure on his skull, as if something was trying to crush it. He craned his neck to try and see behind them. It was almost impossible to read the scanner, but even then, it was no help. It wasn't functioning. Then Starbuck saw it.

A huge ship, a dazzling mass of light moving up behind them and taking position directly overhead. It was gargantuan. Starbuck had never seen anything so large in his entire life. It looked like a planet moving under its own power. The pressure became greater.

"The controls are freezing up," Starbuck shouted, vainly

trying to get the shuttle to respond. "See if you can hit manual override! Sheba! *Sheba!*"

She had collapsed in her seat. Her body slumped forward over the control console. Grimacing with pain, Starbuck reached out and tried to shake her, but could get no response from her. The pain became unbearable. Starbuck released the useless controls and wrapped his arms around his head, as if to block off whatever it was the huge ship was attacking them with. He opened his mouth to scream, but no sound came forth. His eyes rolled up and he collapsed into blackness.

There was a vast expanse of ceiling overhead, made up of irregular, bright chips of some sort that pulsed with a brilliant glow. Starbuck blinked against the light. It was very silent, wherever he was. He stiffened as several faces drifted into view. They were tall and thin. Several of them were leaning over him, gazing down at him. He seemed to be lying on some sort of table. There was nothing restraining him that he could see or feel, but he found that he was unable to move.

Starbuck squinted at the faces of the beings looking down at him. They seemed to give off a light, or to reflect it. They were very white and their features were impossible to discern. All Starbuck could see were startlingly blue eyes located where human eyes should be, except these eyes glowed and were *all* blue, no white, no pupils.

Starbuck licked his lips. They felt very dry. He opened his mouth to speak, but found that it was difficult to get the words out. The first few sounds he made were croaks and wheezes.

"What . . . what is this place?" he finally managed to say. "Who are you?"

"Do not attempt to communicate. You are safe."

He thought, at first, that one of the strange beings had spoken to him, but then he realized that he had heard no sound. The "voice" came to him in his mind, like a thought. It did not have a sound or tone to it, there was nothing Starbuck could discern about it that could identify it as being male or female, if indeed such identification were applicable. It was simply an awareness. The most intimate sort of communication he had ever experienced. It was gentle and soothing.

He started to sit up, struggling against whatever unseen force held him down. It was like moving through water. He seemed to float up rather than sit up, with an effort. He realized that he was naked.

"Sheba—"

One of the beings reached out and Starbuck felt it touch his forehead. It was not a human touch, Starbuck did not feel flesh against his skin. The touch of the bright being was like a gentle warmth against his skin. All the tension left his muscles and he found himself sinking back down onto the surface of the "table" he was lying upon, although he did not feel as though he was lying on a hard surface.

"His restons are normal and responding to balcon infusion."

Again, Starbuck was aware of the communication. The "words" manifested themselves in his mind, though he did not understand them. The terms meant nothing to him.

"Allow him to rise."

They were different "voices." The beings were convers-

ing with each other and Starbuck was aware of their conversation, but he was able to identify the different voices
only because they felt somehow different in his mind. He
could not tell which of the voices belonged to which of the
beings surrounding him. As he gazed at them, trying to
ignore the brightness of them, one of them reached out again
and once again Starbuck felt the touch as a pleasant warmth
upon his skin. The being motioned Starbuck to rise and the
pilot found that he could do so with no difficulty. He tried
to look around him, to see what sort of place he was in, but
the light was devastating. It was like trying to stare directly
at a sun going nova. He had to keep shutting his eyes.

"Who are you?" Starbuck said. "*What* are you? Where's
Sheba?"

"*The companion you refer to will join you as soon as
she is able.*"

Starbuck stood up and took several steps. None of them
tried to stop him. There was something underneath his feet,
some sort of floor, but he could not feel a hard surface.

"What do you mean, as soon as she is able?" he said.
"What have you done to her?"

"*Please be patient.*" He heard, or rather felt, another of
the beings communicating with him telepathically. "*Your
systems are not in phase with our environment. We are
attempting to equalize the forces to a level you can tolerate.*"

"Where are we?" Starbuck said.

"*Within a dimension quite apart from your own.*"

"But I can see you," Starbuck said. "And I can hear
you . . . sort of."

"*That is by our choice.*"

"Really?" Starbuck said. "Well, I'm sure I can—"

He swept his arm out at the nearest of the tall bright

beings and felt heat upon his skin as his hand passed right through the being's body. Starbuck stepped back and stared at his hand. It seemed to be unhurt.

"I couldn't feel—my hand passed right through you!"

A "door" seemed to open somewhere. An area to his right grew brighter and he could see a figure appear, as if out of nowhere. He squinted, trying to see.

"Starbuck?"

It was Sheba. She ran to him and came into his arms. She, too, was naked. She felt warm, warmer than normal body temperature, but there was no perspiration upon her. She seemed to be unhurt.

"Are you all right?" said Starbuck.

"I don't know," said Sheba. "Starbuck, I think maybe we're dead."

Starbuck considered the possibility. The place that they were in was like nothing he had ever seen or heard of. The voice in his mind spoke of being in another dimension. He remembered being in the shuttle, being under some sort of attack, feeling an indescribable agony and then . . . what? Dying? He did not remember dying. But what did it feel like to die? The Book of Kobol spoke of an afterlife, of bright, shimmering beings from another dimension. Starbuck felt afraid.

"Is that right?" he said, not sure he really wanted an answer. "Is it true? We're dead and you're angels?"

Two of the beings exchanged looks.

"Oddly enough," came the voice in his mind, and Sheba seemed to hear it, too, *"there is some truth to your speculation. It is time. Please follow me."*

The beings beckoned to them.

"What do we do?" said Sheba.

Starbuck suspected that there was nothing they could do except as they were told. "Lady," he said to Sheba, "there aren't many places I've been in my life where I didn't feel like I was in complete control. This," he shook his head slowly from side to side, "this is an exception."

They walked slowly, following the glowing creatures. Their eyes no longer hurt quite so much from the brilliance of their mysterious environment. Evidently, the creatures had, as they said, done something to "equalize the forces" to a level they could tolerate, but it was still difficult for them to see clearly. Everything around them shimmered with an opalescent glow. They could discern no shadows and the dimensions of the chambers they were in, if chambers they were, could not be assessed. It was like walking on the floor of some vast milky ocean with the visibility limited to several feet, and that not clearly.

What amazed Starbuck most of all was the complete absence of sound. Part of his cadet training at the academy had required that he spend periods of time in sensory deprivation. A pilot in a disabled Viper fighter drifting through space would easily be subjected to a similar state, a state that would be even more closely related to the training should some injury or other occurrence either blind the pilot or affect visibility. Starbuck had not liked the sensory deprivation training, no pilot had. Inevitably, it resulted in hallucinations and dissociation. The total absence of sound manifested itself as a "heard" phenomenon, a sort of distant roaring echo that could become maddening. Yet, in spite of the fact that there were no sounds of engines of any sort or cooling fans, and their feet made no sounds upon the peculiar surface upon which they walked, Starbuck literally heard nothing. Absolutely nothing. He could not even hear the sound of his own breathing. When he and Sheba spoke to each other, something about their environment gave their words a diffuse, brittle sound that was so surreal that they hesitated to speak needlessly. Their voices did not sound like their own voices. It was, to say the least, an unsettling experience. Starbuck wondered if, perhaps, they really were dead. Everything around them had a mystifying, dreamlike quality.

Before them, once again, they perceived an aperture of some sort that looked like an even brighter wash of light amid an already blindingly brilliant glow. It was as if, staring at a sun, a thin vertical line of greater intensity grew into a quickly expanding ellipsoid. The phenomenon occurred a short distance in front of them and, as before, Starbuck saw a figure silhouetted in the greater brightness. This figure, unlike Sheba's, when she had appeared, was not standing. It was a humanoid shape that appeared to be floating motionless in midair, horizontally.

Starbuck heard the dry, brittle sound of Sheba's voice as she uttered an exclamation of surprise. Then there was the curious sensation of warmth upon their naked backs, the gentle touch of the strange beings urging them forward. They walked through the portal of light, approaching the horizontal figure.

It was Apollo.

His body was not suspended in midair, as had at first appeared, but lying upon a pedestal that blended in, as did everything else around them, with the white glowing background.

"I'd hoped that it was all some horrible dream," said

Sheba. "But it's true. We lived it all."

"What are you doing with him?" Starbuck said to the creatures. "Can't you leave him alone? He's of no possible harm to you."

"Precisely the opposite," said a voice within their minds. *"He is of great value to us."*

"What?" said Starbuck.

"He, and any like him who have the courage to grow beyond the limitations of your evolution."

"What are they saying?" Sheba said.

"I don't know."

"Starbuck, you have a most promising spirit. A trifle unrestrained, but perhaps with Apollo's continued fellowship—"

"Please don't," said Sheba. "I've lived through his death once. Don't keep reminding me of what I brought about."

"Apollo was not meant to die. It was you that Diabolis meant to destroy."

"A lot of good that does now," said Starbuck. "What difference does it make? Are we supposed to feel better about Apollo's death knowing that it was an accident?"

"Apollo sacrificed his mortal body to save your spirit from falling. Are you willing to sacrifice your own to bring him back?"

"Look," said Starbuck, "whatever you are, we've been through enough. Whatever you're going to do with us, get it over with."

"Yes," said Sheba. "If it's possible, I would do anything."

"Sheba," Starbuck said, "you don't know what you're saying. These creatures could—"

"They're people, Starbuck," she said.

"You're delirious."

"No, I mean it. They are people. They're not unlike us. They don't . . . *feel* different to me. They know what we are, who we are."

"That gives them a pretty big advantage."

"It doesn't matter," she said. "If it's possible to bring him back, if they can do it somehow, I think . . . yes, all right. I will trade my life for Apollo's. *Is* it possible?"

"Many things are possible. What about you, Starbuck? Did you not say inside your ship that you would gladly trade places with Apollo?"

"How could you know that?" said Starbuck.

"Step away."

They were urged back from Apollo's body by a gentle warmth. As they watched, a fine mist seemed to grow around Apollo's body. It emanated from below and above him, gradually cloaking his body and growing thicker. It had a stark purple hue, in violent contrast to everything else around them. The tiny particles washed over Apollo's body, moving with great speed until Apollo was completely hidden from view. There was no sound.

Gradually, the mist began to ebb and fade, falling away from him like the last remnants of a brief summer shower. Apollo's eyelids fluttered. His chest began to rise and fall.

Starbuck and Sheba stared with disbelief as he began to regain consciousness. Slowly, he began to rise up to a sitting position. He did not seem to be puzzled by his surroundings. Starbuck thought that the expression on his face was one of complete tranquility. He looked serene.

Sheba cried out and ran to him. They embraced.

Starbuck turned to the shining aliens.

"I don't know who you are," he said, "but whatever you want from me, you can have."

"We want nothing from you."

"Then, why? Why have you done this?"

"Because we fight a common foe."

"I don't understand," said Starbuck. "You mean Diabolis? I feel like a fool talking to you. It's like a drone in the presence of its creator. You're playing with us. We're like toys to you."

Starbuck sensed amusement from the beings.

"No. You are wrong. We are not your creators. We are more like your parents. You are barely born, barely able to move about. You are as capable of harming yourselves and others as you are of giving love."

"Then why bother with us?" Starbuck said.

"Because we love you. We want you to grow and learn. And to help others as we have helped you."

Sheba and Apollo approached and Starbuck turned to them with tears in his eyes. He looked at Apollo and smiled, wiping at his eyes.

"It must be all this light," he said.

The two men embraced, holding each other tightly as if to assure each other that they were real.

"I don't think I've ever felt anything like this before in my entire life," said Starbuck.

"I know," Apollo said, smiling. "It's like love. Pure love. And we've been in its presence."

"Who's going to believe this?" Sheba said.

Starbuck began to laugh. Sheba and Apollo joined in, feeling uncontrollably giddy and overcome with joy.

* * *

The shuttle settled to the deck of the landing bay aboard the *Battlestar Galactica*. As Apollo, Starbuck and Sheba climbed out, they were met by Adama, Athena, Cassiopea, Boxey and his droid and Boomer. It was like a family reunion.

"Boomer!" said Apollo. "I don't believe it!"

"I hardly believe it myself," said Boomer, hugging his friend.

"I thought we'd lost you," said Apollo. "The other pilots? Any sign of them?"

"All safe," said Adama. "And apparently the victims of the same thing, some kind of navigational pilfering at the hands of Count Iblis."

"I don't understand," said Starbuck.

"Their ships started sending out distress signals from that burned-out planet where you found Count Iblis," said Athena.

"We sent out a patrol and, sure enough, every one of our warriors was there, waiting," Adama said. "They were out of fuel, but otherwise perfectly fine. We also picked up Sheba's Viper. But what about *you?* We'd almost given up hope. You were the ones we expected to find on that planet, not the missing pilots."

"It's been quite an experience," Apollo said, "and it isn't easy to explain. I wonder if we could tell you about it a little more privately?"

"Of course," Adama said. "You must be exhausted. We'll have some food. We'll have a feast!"

* * *

They sat around a table in Adama's quarters. The lighting was subdued as they drank ambrosa. Adama raised his goblet in a toast.

"To the return of our children," he said, "and the end of Count Iblis, whoever he was."

Apollo frowned. Sheba and Starbuck, likewise, suddenly appeared confused.

Adama resumed his seat after they all drank.

"According to Doctor Paye in the life station," said Adama, "you found Count Iblis back on the surface of that planet. Was that correct?"

"That's right," said Apollo.

"Yet, you don't seem to know where he went."

Apollo shrugged. "Father, it's like those ships of light that come and go in the wink of an eye."

"That's right," said Sheba. "One micron, he was standing there and the next, he simply vanished."

"Then what happened?" said Athena. "Why weren't you there when we found the rest of the pilots?"

"Yes, why?" said Boomer. "We didn't find any sign of you and if you had headed straight back toward the fleet, how did we get here before you?"

"Something happened down on that planet," Starbuck said slowly. He tried to remember, but it wasn't clear. The memory seemed to hover somewhere on the edge of his consciousness, but he couldn't dredge it up. "Something happened and I just can't explain it," he finished lamely, wondering why he could not remember.

Adama looked to his son. "Apollo?"

Apollo shook his head. "I don't know. I can't remember anything after challenging Count Iblis."

"You challenged him and won," Adama said. "That confirms he was a charlatan."

"No, Adama," Sheba said. "Apollo challenged him and lost."

"Lost?" Adama stared at her, not comprehending. "But how do you mean that?"

"What she means," said Starbuck, "is that Count Iblis tried to kill Sheba and Apollo got in his way."

"That's the last thing I remember," said Apollo.

Adama was confused. "Sheba? Starbuck?"

"No, no, wait," said Starbuck. "I remember a little more. I remember Sheba and I taking Apollo's body aboard the shuttle and leaving the planet."

"And next you landed aboard the *Galactica*," Adama said. "Obviously Apollo was merely stunned and you frightened Count Iblis off."

"I guess that must be it," said Starbuck, "except for—"

"A white light," said Boomer.

Adama glanced at him. "What?"

"A white light," said Boomer. "There was a brilliant white light and some kind of incredible pressure—"

"Yes," said Sheba. "Then you felt it, too!"

Boomer looked puzzled. It was as if, all of a sudden, there were lapses in their memories. The more they tried to think about it, the more difficult it was to recall exactly what had happened. Their food and wine remained untouched upon the table as they looked at each other, wondering why none of them could remember what had happened to them.

"Starbuck?" Boomer said.

Starbuck got up from the table and walked slowly to the

observation port. He looked out at the stars, a faraway look in his eyes.

"Yes," he said, "there *was* something. A light. An incredibly bright light. . . ."

Adama looked toubled. "Don't try to remember now," he said. "It was obviously traumatic. You've been through some kind of horrendous experience."

"No," said Starbuck. "It was beautiful."

Sheba nodded. "Yes, it was."

Apollo got up and walked to the observation port to stand beside Starbuck. For a moment, they stood looking out at the stars in silence.

"There's something out there," said Apollo. He shivered and held his shoulders, folding his arms in front of him. Adama rushed to his side.

"Son, are you all right?"

"I'm fine," Apollo said. He looked at his father and smiled. "Just a little sore, for some reason. Anyway, I guess we're all suffering from a certain amount of battle fatigue. Maybe we're a bit disoriented, but at least we're together and we're alive. And we know where we're going."

"Earth," said Adama.

"Sector Beta," said Apollo. "Nineteen million sectars by—"

"By epsilon vector twenty-two," said Starbuck. "On a course reckoning of 0000 point nine."

"In a star system containing nine planets and a single sun," said Sheba.

"What is this?" said Adama. "How do you know these coordinates, all three of you, practically in unison?"

They looked at him and he saw that they were as mystified about what they had said as he was.

"I don't know, Father," said Apollo. "I have no idea." He turned back to stare out into space.

FROM THE ADAMA JOURNALS:

Part of being a leader is knowing when *not* to tell the people under your command the truth. Count Iblis, whoever or whatever he was, remains a hero to the people in the fleet. We told them that he kept his promise to lead us to the planet Earth by giving us the coordinates that Sheba, Starbuck and Apollo supplied. Between us, we made up a story about those white ships calling him back out to wherever it was he came from. In retrospect, it all sounds pretty foolish, but when people want something badly enough, they'll settle for foolish. Everybody wanted an answer and there was no one around to give them one. I want answers and all I have are questions.

I want to know what sort of creature it was we took on board our ship. It was not human, of that I'm certain. However, knowing human nature as I do, I must admit that I have to consider the possibility that if Count Iblis wasn't human, he was at least related to us somehow. That is not a thought that sits well with me. That thing, whatever it was, knew us and knew us well. I have no doubt that it had spent time on Earth. I only hope the people on Earth were stronger, better able to deal with it than we.

And what of Earth? How did Sheba, Starbuck and Apollo learn of its location? That question, more than any other, troubles me. Something happened out there, something that affected my three warriors in a way that has changed them profoundly. There is a greater degree of introspection in them now. Even in Starbuck, there is less manic intensity. They share more silences together and I sometimes see them exchanging looks that speak of things I'm not sure I would understand.

I had resigned myself to losing my son, to losing all of them. I had done something I had sworn that I would never do, an oath that dates back to the destruction of Caprica and the other colony worlds. I had given up hope. I am not ashamed to admit it, it's what happened and I am responsible for it. I allowed my own fears to stand between me and what I believed. When Iblis said that he would punish me by taking Apollo's life, I had offered up my own, selfishly. And it *was* a selfish action.

I spoke before of heroism. There was no heroism in my offering my life in exchange for Apollo's. Had it been Starbuck or Sheba or Boomer making the offer, the action would have been heroic, but had *my* offer been accepted, it would have been an act of cowardice. What makes me different? I acted out of fear.

I had lost my wife, my home, indeed, my world. I could not bear to also lose my son. To die in Apollo's place would have been easier for me than to live with the fact of my son's death, knowing that I might have prevented it. And I had to live, because of my responsibility. My duty to the fleet came first, but in that moment, I had forgotten it and would have forsaken everything, even my life, to save my son. To save myself from having to live with grief and guilt. I could make it easier on myself and say that I did it out of love. It would be true, since I do love my son, but it would not be the whole truth. My duty may force me to lie to the poeple in the fleet about what happened to Count Iblis, since they need to have their heroes, but I will not lie to myself.

Where there is no data and the questions overwhelm, the mind seeks answers in the most frenetic way, often overlooking facts. I wanted desperately to believe that Count Iblis was a charlatan, that he had duped us all, because to have believed the converse would have been too frightening. I wanted to believe that my son had bested him back on that burned-out red planet. Yet, Starbuck and Sheba were witness to the fact that he did not and I, even with the faith I have in Apollo's abilities, knew that it was true. Apollo would have been no match for Count Iblis.

Yet, Apollo had returned.

Starbuck and Sheba remembered, although they remembered little else, they claimed, seeing him fall. I wish to God I knew what really happened. Because I am certain that someone or something *intervened*.

What happened to those warriors that we lost and later found on that desolate planet? They all claim, to a man, that they were there all the time, waiting for us to come and pick them up. Yet, why is it that we did not start to receive their distress signals until centons after they had disappeared? If they had been there all the time, why did they wait? And why weren't Starbuck, Sheba and Apollo with them? That was where they had gone.

Questions. Questions with no answers. But everything does seem to have one common denominator.

The white lights.

We all saw them. They swarmed around the *Galactica* like insects, moving with impossible speed. Count Iblis seemed to be afraid of them. And each of our pilots remembered seeing an incredibly bright light before they disappeared. And between the time we lost them and the time we started to receive their distress signals, they could not account for what had happened to them. I can speculate about what they might mean, but it would merely be an endless circle. I would never know for sure. I do, however, have my suspicions. The story would have ended there, except there was one grace note.

The night Starbuck, Sheba and Apollo returned to us, there was a feast in my private quarters. It was a small, intimate gathering. My two children were there, Athena and Apollo, along with my adopted children, Starbuck and Sheba. Boomer was there and later, when she got off duty, Cassiopea came to join us, bringing little Boxey with her. We all sat around the table and I was anxious to hear their story.

Except they had no story to tell.

I could see it in their faces. They wanted to tell me what had happened, but it was as if the memory of it all were taken from them somehow, blocked off. At first, I thought that it was shock. The experience had been a traumatic one and they were not quite ready to deal with it yet. In time, it would become easier for them and they would tell me.

It seemed a simple, logical answer. It satisfied me until they told me the way to Earth. There was no way they could have known that. Some sort of psychosis as a result of what they had been through together? Possibly.

We sat together for a long time that night, much of it in silence. It just felt good for all of us to be there. By ones and twos, they eventually drifted off to their own quarters and to their own thoughts, leaving me with mine. I was weary and wanted nothing so much as to sleep.

That night, I had a dream.

The *Galactica* was once again surrounded by the swarming lights. They darted around the ship, hurtled through the fleet like some ghostly meteor shower. I knew that they were there, but I was powerless to act. I heard Colonel Tigh calling me from the bridge, but I could not open my eyes, much less get out of bed. Powerless to move, I heard the red alert claxon reverberating throughout the ship. I heard the pilots rushing by outside my door, running to the launch tubes, but by the time they were ready to launch, the white lights were gone. They did not come back. I was never to see them again.

Sometime during that surreal vision, I heard a voice. At first, I thought someone was speaking to me, but then I realized that the voice I was hearing was in my mind. I wasn't hearing anything at all. It was as though I was thinking someone else's thoughts.

The voice spoke of human fallibility. It spoke of revenge and of how not even the avenger is immune from that which he exacts. It spoke of making a bad bargain, of owing something to a force which did not forget debts that were incurred. And it spoke of order and of balance. I do not recall the words it used if, indeed, it did use words. I only know that after I experienced having that presence in my mind, I fell into a deep and dreamless sleep.

When I awoke, I learned that we were short one prisoner.

CHAPTER TEN

Baltar sat alone upon the floor in a solitary confinement
cubicle and wept. It was over, finished. His glorious dream
of ruling a world for the Cylon Empire would be nothing
more than that, a dream. He had sacrificed everything,
everything in order to achieve his goal and now it was out
of his reach forever.

He had helped the Cylons to destroy twelve worlds in
order to get what he wanted and he had thrown it all away.
Why? What had possessed him to leave the safety of his
base ship and fly to Adama? What made him think that his
worst enemy would even consider a truce with the one man
he hated above all others? He was a traitor to the human
race. He had become so willingly. He had planned to sell
out the Council of the Twelve so that the Cylons could
conquer. What madness induced him to believe that they
would ever forget what he had done? He, Baltar, honored

nothing, held nothing sacred. Why should they have honored his offer of a truce?

He could not blame Adama. Ironically, for the first time in his life, Adama had acted as Baltar would have acted. Had Adama come to Baltar with an offer of a truce, Baltar would have done exactly as Adama had with him. No, Baltar thought, perhaps not. Probably not. He would have made sure that Adama died. Slowly and unpleasantly.

They had put him in solitary aboard the prison ship. To risk putting him in with any of the other prisoners meant his death. Those thrown into the brig by Adama and the council had no reason to love either, but they had even less reason to love Baltar. They would have torn him to shreds with their bare hands. When he was brought to the prison ship, news of his capture had already reached the inmates. As he was being taken to his cell, he heard their cries and threats and it had chilled him to the bone. They had yelled for blood. His blood.

The sentence was life imprisonment. It might have been kinder to simply kill him. How long could he possibly survive in a tiny cubicle, in solitary, without even a machine like Lucifer to talk to? How long would it be before he lost his sanity? Not long. It was that which frightened Baltar more than anything else. He imagined himself a mindless vegetable, crawling around upon the floor and making whimpering sounds and soiling himself. This, the would-be ruler of a world.

The final blow had been that they had given him a cell with an observation port. He could hammer upon it for the remainder of his life and he would not so much as scratch it, yet he would be able to see the outside. He would be able to see the stars. He would know that somewhere out there was the base ship he had commanded. The ship that would not give up the chase simply because he had disappeared. No, it would be assumed that he had died and the hunt would continue and, one day, the base ship that had once been his would find the *Battlestar Galactica* and destroy her. And he would be on board, watching it all happen. He didn't want to die, but he knew that it would not be long before he would dream of it.

Baltar wrapped his arms around his head and huddled against the wall, weeping.

"It can't end like this," he moaned. "Please, don't let it end like this."

Something flashed by outside. A white flaring through the observation port made him look up. He ran to the port and looked outside.

The ship was surrounded by white lights. He heard the red alert signal sound. Outside and above his observation port, from an angle that he could not see, a brighter light was growing closer. Baltar backed away in fear.

Suddenly he felt incredible pain, as if a tremendous blow had been delivered to his head, resulting in a massive edema. He clutched at his head, doubling over with pain. It kept increasing. Baltar screamed.

He awoke in the life station. At first, he thought he was being treated aboard the *Galactica* or possibly the prison ship, then he saw a Cylon med tech looking down at him. He was in a life pod and his vital signs were being monitored.

"What—where am I?" he said, looking around him and seeing several other Cylons in the life station. Had they captured the fleet? Could it be?

"You are aboard the base ship, Baltar."

He looked up and saw Lucifer gliding toward him across the floor, moving with his usual soundless grace.

"Lucifer!" He struggled to sit up. "What happened? How did I get here?"

"You do not recall?" said Lucifer.

Baltar looked at the I.L. series Cylon and shook his head.

"We received your distress signal," Lucifer said. "I dispatched a patrol to investigate and they found your shuttle, drifting in space. You were aboard, but you were not conscious. At first, they thought that you were dead. Did you not find the *Galactica?*"

Baltar slowly climbed out of the life pod. His whole body felt sore, though why he did not know.

"The *Galactica?*" he said.

"Yes," said Lucifer. "You were to rendezvous with the *Battlestar Galactica*. You departed in the shuttle alone, unescorted."

"Rendezvous with the *Galactica?*" Baltar stared at Lucifer as if the computer had gone insane. *"Alone?* Why in the name of Kobol would I do anything as mad as that?"

Lucifer stood silent, his red eyes appraising Baltar. "It was by your order," he finally said.

Baltar turned away. *"My* order? Impossible. I do not remember giving any such order."

He tried to remember. What was he doing alone in a shuttle that was drifting out in space? How did he get there? *Why* was it all a total blank?

"Was I ill?" he asked Lucifer.

"Your bodily functions are all normal. Nor were you ill before you left. What happened out there, Baltar? Did you find Adama?"

"Adama?" Baltar shook his head. "No. No, I—I don't remember."

"Baltar, we must—"

"Leave me."

Lucifer hesitated, as if about to say something else. "By your command," he said, then turned and silently left the life station.

Baltar sat down, rubbing his temples. His head ached, his whole body ached. How could he have blanked out so completely?

"The *Galactica*," he said softly to himself. There was something about the *Battlestar Galactica*. But what? He tried to concentrate, but all that he could manage to summon up were fleeting images.

Alone, in a shuttle. *Why? Going where?*

Adama, and a stranger, a tall stranger dressed in white flowing robes.

Alone again, in some sort of small chamber.

"A dream," said Baltar. "It must have been a dream."

But it was not a dream. They had found him drifting out in space. Alone. And he remembered nothing. Nothing.

"It isn't finished," he said to himself. "It isn't finished, after all."

He frowned. Why would he say something like that? Of course it wasn't finished. It would not be finished until he had tracked Adama down, until he had destroyed the accursed *Battlestar Galactica* and her pathetic fleet. They were out there somewhere and, sooner or later, he would find them again and finish it once and for all.

Baltar leaned forward, putting his head in his hands.

"Why can't I remember?" he said. *"Why?"*

He felt that if he could only concentrate, he could bring

it back, but try as he might, nothing but faint images tantalized his mind, images that didn't seem to mean anything. He could make no sense out of them. One image in particular disturbed him greatly.

He seemed to remember a white light. An incredibly bright white light. . . .

14

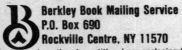

MS READ-a-thon— a simple way to start youngsters reading

Boys and girls between 6 and 14 can join the MS READ-a-thon and help find a cure for Multiple Sclerosis by reading books. And they get two rewards — the enjoyment of reading, and the great feeling that comes from helping others.

Parents and educators: For complete information call your local MS chapter. Or mail the coupon below.

Kids can help, too!